OTHER
Harlequin Romances
by MARY BURCHELL

Elusive Harmony

by

MARY BURCHELL

Harlequin Books

TORONTO • LONDON • NEW YORK • AMSTERDAM • SYDNEY • WINNIPEG

Original hardcover edition published in 1976
by Mills & Boon Limited

ISBN 0-373-02043-0

Harlequin edition published February 1977

Printed in Canada

CHAPTER ONE

'SOMEONE will have to tell him.' Charles Drury scribbled an aimless line or two on the pad in front of him and then looked up at the girl who was standing very still by the window. 'Do you want me to do it?'

'No.' She moved at last and shook her head. 'It's better I should. A humiliation comes better from a daughter, I suppose, than from even the most devoted of secretaries.'

'You think he'll take it badly?'

'Of course he'll take it badly! Even at fifty-four'—automatically Natalie took five years off her father's age—'and with years of honour and glory behind him, he's still like a child in his love of his position.'

'We-ell——' Charles Drury rubbed his chin meditatively. 'If you've been one of'—he corrected himself quickly—'if you've been the greatest tenor in the world for a couple of decades it isn't easy to have to step down.'

'He hasn't done that yet,' she countered sharply. And then, as there was silence from her companion, she said sadly, 'I sometimes think the audience have the best of it. The artists have so much anguish as well as joy and triumph.'

'Both have their compensations,' Charles replied. 'The people who have the worst of it are the poor wretches who have to act as the buffer between the artists and the public.'

'And that's you and me?' she smiled ruefully and he thought how attractively those smoky blue eyes of hers lit up when she did that.

'More you than me,' he conceded. 'I do have some sort of regular hours. Within limits,' he added with a grimace as he reflected on the charming, insistent demands which his employer could make upon him. 'But for you it's twenty-four hours out of twenty-four, isn't it? Does it never occur to you that perhaps you're wasting your life, Natalie?'

'Yes,' she said unexpectedly. 'There are times when it seems to me that time is rushing past and I am standing still, but there isn't much else I can do. He's so utterly dependent on me in so many ways.'

'Isn't that taking daughterly devotion too far?' Charles sounded a trifle impatient.

She smiled and shook her head. 'It wasn't I who started it, you know. My mother did. And by the time I came into the picture he was so set in his ways—so utterly dependent on someone to cherish and support and reassure him—that it would have been like taking away a prop from a magnificent building and leaving it to crumble, if I hadn't stepped into the breach.'

'Was that how it was? I've sometimes wondered. I didn't know your mother, of course. She died the year before I came to work for your father.'

'She was,' said Natalie Harding slowly, 'the most amazing person. Astonishingly beautiful and attractive and vital in her own right, but completely satisfied to

6

put all her gifts at his disposal. She adored him. And, to be perfectly fair, he adored her too, and was as proud of her as if he'd invented her himself.'

'And you?' Charles Drury asked drily. 'Where did you come in the picture?'

'Oh——' Natalie frowned thoughtfully and then said, entirely without rancour, 'I was almost incidental, I suppose. They were both fond of me in an absent-minded sort of way, but I'm sure they forgot my very existence for days on end when I was at school. Artists are like that.'

'But she wasn't an artist,' he protested.

'No. But she was a sort of extension of him. She almost literally lived in and for him. There are always sacrifices involved, I suppose, if you are helping to make a great artist.'

'It's monstrous!' He sounded genuinely angry.

'Of course it is.' She laughed, this time with real amusement. 'But the compensations are terrific—when everything goes well. I once heard someone say that great artists tend to be half genius and half monster. I wouldn't go as far as that. But they do things one couldn't accept in ordinary people and then, just as you could kill them, they lift you out of the humdrum world of reality in such a way that you could adore them. My father could do just that. *You* know it as well as I do.'

He nodded wordlessly. And after a moment she said, almost as though she could not help it, 'He can still do it.—*Can't* he?'

'Yes,' Charles Drury agreed slowly, 'he can still do it. But not so frequently and not so—reliably. That's why he isn't being offered the lead in this new work.'

She shivered involuntarily.

'I imagine your mother never had to deal with a situation like this,' he said reflectively. 'In her time it was one long string of successes, wasn't it?'

'Oh, yes! All the world was their gorgeous, glittering stage, and I'm not being prejudiced when I say they adorned it superbly. It wasn't only the glamour and the money and the intoxication of success. They were such *artists* in everything they did. He lived for music and the perfecting of his God-given talents, and she lived for him and everything he stood for. And then, quite suddenly—she died.' Natalie made an expressive gesture with her hands, and it occurred to Charles Drury that she had inherited something of her father's genius for conveying everything with the simplest of movements.

'It was in my last few weeks at school,' she recalled musingly. 'I was sent for, and I came home to find him in total collapse. It must have seemed to him that the sun had been put out and the birds had ceased to sing. I remember thinking, "Do people literally die of a broken heart? and is that what is going to happen to him?" It was Oscar Warrender—the famous conductor, you know—who almost tore him out of the slough of despond. He invented some frightful dilemma, in which only my father could get them out of a casting difficulty. He came across the Atlantic himself and fetched him. And I went too.

'It was several years since my father had sung at the Met and so it wasn't so full of agonising memories of

8

Mother as some other places. I did what I could—comforting him, supporting him, filling her place in some small degree. And Warrender of course was marvellous. It ended in Father scoring one of the greatest artistic triumphs of his life, and at the end he had found his new offstage rôle. He was no longer the golden tenor with the world his plaything, he was the great artist who had known tragedy and could therefore interpret everything afresh.'

'You said that entirely without sarcasm, didn't you?' Charles cocked an amused eyebrow at her.

'Of course.' Natalie looked faintly surprised. 'It's the truth.'

'That he plays a rôle offstage as well as on? Doesn't that make you put your tongue in your cheek a little?'

'No. That's how God made him. It's as much part of him as his heavenly voice. Who am I to criticise?'

'Well, that's one way of looking at it, I suppose.' Charles conceded with a laugh. 'Your father is a lucky man. In so far as he has you, I mean,' he added rather awkwardly as he remembered the shock in store for his employer.

'I wish Dermot Deane had waited to tell him until we got back to London,' Natalie said with a sigh. 'Why did he have to send a letter after him to Germany? It's been such a happy tour. Particularly the concert last night.'

'Perhaps that will soften the blow,' suggested Charles.

'No, it will highlight the insult,' retorted Natalie. 'For that's how he'll regard it, you know.' She went over to the window again and stood looking down into the sunny, tree-lined street of this charming German town, which had once been a ducal preserve and even now retained something of the provincial elegance of earlier days.

'He's coming now,' she said softly. 'You'd better go, Charles.' And as she stood watching her tall, handsome father stop by an ornamental fountain to address a few smiling, gracious words to a group of children playing there, she heard Charles go out, closing the door after him.

Kind Charles! devoted Charles, who ably shouldered so much of the actual work involved in her father's career. But when it came to something personal and basic like this, there was only Natalie to deal with it. She wondered how her mother would have tackled it. Had it really been roses and triumphs all the way for her? or had she too sometimes had to deal with seeming disaster and humiliation?

That was the word which stuck in one's throat. It would be such humiliation for him to be set aside for a younger man, when all the indications had been that he could expect this new, important rôle to be his almost by right of his position in the operatic world.

'It's not just vanity and pride, in the petty sense,' she thought, almost as though she were trying to convince someone else of the truth of this. 'He has been at the top—and deservedly so—for half his professional life. He'd be a fool if, artist that he is, he couldn't assess his own real worth.' And her father was anything but a fool, she knew, so far as his art was concerned.

But in every career of this sort a time had to come which was like the striking of midnight to Cinderella. The first chill, unmistakable sign that the glory was about to depart. Or at least to be dimmed.

She turned as the door opened and her father entered, and she thought for the thousandth time how splendid he was to look at. He never just came into a room, like other people. He quite simply made an entrance, without fuss or any exaggeration of movement, just as he came on to a stage and immediately reduced everyone else to lesser importance. A few of the very greatest have this quality, which is something one can neither teach nor learn. Drama flows naturally outward from them and where they stand there is the centre of the stage. Those who have it in any one period can usually be counted on the fingers of one hand.

'It's a wonderful afternoon,' observed Lindley Harding, and immediately the conventional statement took on a special depth of meaning, so that the beauty of the afternoon followed him into the hotel sitting-room as an almost living thing.

'Yes,' said his daughter inadequately. And then, as he crossed to the desk, 'Father, there's a letter from Dermot Deane. I opened it in case it was something urgent.'

'Quite right,' replied her father, who was almost uniformly bored by the business side of his career. 'Had he anything important to say?'

This was the moment, and Natalie drew a deep breath.

'Most of it was unimportant——'

'Dermot has a genius for noting trivialities, dear fellow,' observed her father indulgently.

'But he does write quite positively about the casting for Beverley Caine's new opera.'

'Oh, yes?' The well-shaped hand which had been extended towards the desk was suddenly arrested, in a moment of stillness which was almost heart-stopping in its eloquence.

'The principal tenor rôle has gone to Laurence Morven.'

'I've never heard of him,' said Lindley Harding coldly, in a tone which consigned the gentleman to total obscurity.

'Oh, Father, you must have! He made a great success in *Andréa Chénier* at San Francisco, and——'

'I don't follow the careers of secondary artists,' replied her father simply. 'How came the management to make such a mistake? That rôle requires an artist of maturity and experience. In the hands of a beginner——'

'I don't think anyone could call Laurence Morven a beginner,' Natalie interrupted unhappily. 'He——'

'Have you heard him?'

'No, of course not. You know I haven't.'

'Then don't offer an opinion upon him,' said her father, apparently unaware that he was doing exactly that himself. 'I suppose he has youth on his side.' He curled his handsome mouth with an air that had made him a matchless Don Carlos in his time. 'Youth!' he repeated the word as though it were a prime insult. 'I presume he can gallop about the stage making himself ridiculous and leap up and down the staircases so beloved of modern producers. The idea is preposterous. Get Dermot on the telephone for me.'

'He won't be in his office on a Saturday afternoon.'

'Then get him at his home. And don't make silly objections, Natalie. You know they make me nervous and irritable.'

Natalie went through all the necessary motions, hoping cravenly that her father's agent would be out of England, or at least engaged elsewhere. But within a few minutes she heard his cheerful voice say, 'Dermot Deane here.'

'Oh, Mr Deane, it's Natalie Harding. My father——'

The receiver was gently but firmly removed from her hand and her father, leaning against the desk with extraordinary grace for a man of his age, said, 'What is this nonsense, Dermot, about the casting of Kit Marlowe in the new Beverley Caine opera?'

There was a slight pause, then Natalie heard her father say smoothly, 'Don't speak so fast, my dear fellow. All I need are the simple facts.'

After which—and before his agent at the other end of the wire could give any more simple facts—he went on to analyse the part in detail, explaining why it was quite impossible that anyone other than himself could sing the rôle.

'What's that you say?—That I have everything required for the part?—Well, it isn't for me to say so, but since you put it that way—Except what? I can't hear you. Except *youth*? My dear chap, youth isn't what is needed for this part of Kit Marlowe. What?—Yes, of course I know Marlowe died young, historically speaking. But what has that to do with opera? Salome was sixteen, come to that, when she started cutting capers for the head of John the Baptist; but that hasn't prevented many a soprano of forty puffing her way through the Dance of the Seven Veils.—That isn't the same thing? Well, it damn well nearly is, you know.'

As far as Natalie could judge, Dermot Deane cut in with some determination at this point because her father was obviously constrained to listen. And, glancing at him anxiously, she saw that the indulgent smile had faded from his face and that the faint lines round his handsome eyes had deepened.

Finally, he said rather heavily, though still with a note of incredulity in his expressive voice, 'You mean it's all *settled*?'

Apparently it was all settled, because he was silent again for nearly a minute. Then he seemed to draw an almost tangible cloak of dignity round him as he observed, 'Then there's nothing more for me to say. Except that I'm sorry—I'm very sorry indeed—to think that poor Beverley Caine's fine work is doomed to failure even before it goes into rehearsal.'

On this splendid valedictory remark he replaced the telephone. But Natalie was shocked and dismayed to see that his hand was trembling so much that he actually rattled the receiver on its stand.

She had never known such a thing happen before. Like most fine stage artists, her father was in superb command of his nerves and muscles. Even in the worst days, after the death of her mother and during the

14

emotional collapse which followed, his step had remained firm and his carriage upright. She had never seen his hand tremble even then. And now it was shaking like—like the hand of an old man.

The comparison came unbidden to her mind, and gave her the sharpest sense of pity and dismay she had ever known.

'I'm so sorry, darling.' She came over to him, as he sank down into an armchair, and put her hand on his shoulder. 'I know it's dreadfully disappointing. But there are so many other rôles——'

'It's not for myself I'm distressed.' He seemed quite unaware that this was palpably untrue. 'I'm grieved—yes, truly grieved—for poor Caine.'

Natalie was silent, feeling virtually certain that poor Caine had been one of those most eager to have the young, much-praised Laurence Morven for his work. Then with tact and skill—and long experience—she exerted herself to make just the right amount and type of conversation needed to raise her father's spirits. She referred, though almost passingly, to various successes of his, lingering for some moments on his remarkable triumph in the concert of the previous evening.

Presently he said he thought he would rest for a while. And he went into his bedroom, leaving Natalie to wonder if the worst were over, or if in actual fact he simply had to be alone with the raw realisation that for certain rôles he was apparently no longer the top choice.

She sought out Charles, gave him a brief account of what had happened, and then, released from the immediate pressure of her responsibilities, she went out of the hotel for half an hour of blessed solitude in the small nearby park which had once been the gardens of the ducal residence.

It was soothingly peaceful, strolling along through alternating sunshine and shade, and she was glad to reflect that, as she and her father were not flying back home until the next day, even the minor problem of packing need not be dealt with urgently. If he really were going to take this unexpected rebuff fairly well, it might prove to be a relatively painless first step away from the full noonday sun of his brilliant career. If, on the other hand——

She never got as far as formulating the alternative, because at that moment a loutish youth on a fast bicycle came charging out of a side turning, caught her a glancing blow, saw that though she staggered she had not actually fallen and, calling back a casual apology in German, rode on.

Natalie stood for a moment where she was, all her resolution required not to keel over as an agonisingly sharp pain in her left ankle made it impossible to set that foot to the ground. Then an elderly woman came up to her and took her by the arm, all the while pouring out a flood of German, expressive of sympathy with Natalie and fury with the vanished cause of the trouble.

'I can't—walk——' stammered Natalie. Then she repeated that in halting German and the woman said sympathetically, '*Engländerin!*' and clicked her tongue, as though that made the dilemma even worse. Which, of course, in a way it did.

'I can't just go on standing here like a stork,' thought

Natalie, and laughed weakly at her own thoughts, thereby evidently suggesting to her anxious companion that she might lapse into hysterics.

'Ah!' The German woman gave an exclamation of relief, as a tall, fair-haired man came into view, and she called to him to come to their assistance.

He came at once, answered her in fluent German and then, having gathered that the poor injured young lady was English, he said, 'Well, that's all right. I'm English too. At least, English-speaking. Here, let's get you to a seat.' And without much apparent difficulty, he picked up Natalie and carried her to a nearby seat under the trees and set her down there.

The German woman, evidently feeling that Natalie was now in good hands, said something about being late already, gave the younger woman a pat on the shoulder and took herself off.

'What happened exactly?' the man wanted to know. And when Natalie had explained he said in a concerned tone, 'It isn't broken, is it?'

'Oh, no!' she cried, dismayed at the thought of all the complications that would involve. 'No, he caught me a crack with one of his pedals, I think, and I wrenched my ankle as I tried to regain my balance. It—it will be all right in a minute or two, I expect.'

'It won't, you know.' He looked down at her swelling ankle, and then up again into her face, and she thought what remarkable eyes he had. Clear grey, astonishingly well set in a suntanned face and unexpectedly fringed with thick black lashes. 'Sit there for a minute,' he told her, 'and then I'll see about getting you back to wherever you're staying.'

'It's very kind of you.' To her surprise, her voice actually quivered slightly, partly from pain and shock and partly because it was a long while since anyone had volunteered so naturally to look after her. 'Do—do you live here?' she added, quickly covering her emotion with a conventional question.

'No, I'm here for only a couple of days,' he explained. 'I came to hear a concert, as a matter of fact, because——'

'The recital last night?' Her voice lightened on a pleased note.

'Yes. Were you there?' He looked interested.

'I was.' She smiled. 'How did you like it?'

'Immensely, of course.' He was pleasingly emphatic about that. But then he went on, 'The old boy's a sort of miracle. He can still pull out most of the stops, though he must be sixty if he's a day.'

'He is fifty-four, as a matter of fact,' Natalie stated coolly. 'I should know. I'm his daughter.'

'Oh, lord! I'm sorry.' He looked taken aback, but rather amused too.

'It's all right.' Her tone was still cold. 'The public often make mistakes like that. What they don't know about famous people they tend to invent.'

'No doubt you're right,' he agreed, 'but I wasn't deliberately inventing, you know.'

'I'm sure you weren't,' she replied quickly, suddenly recalling how kind he had been to a complete stranger. 'I think I'm being specially touchy at the moment. You see'—afterwards she supposed it was just because

18

they *were* complete strangers that she took him into her confidence in such an inexplicable manner—'you see, his age has just been called in question over an important piece of casting. He's been put aside for some unimportant young tenor about half his age and probably with a tenth of his artistry.'

'I—see,' said the young man. Then, glancing down at her ankle again, he exclaimed, 'I think I must get you back to your hotel as quickly as possible now. You should have a doctor to see that. You sit here and I'll go to the gate and get a taxi. The man can drive along that main path as far as this seat, then I can easily carry you to the taxi and see you to your hotel.'

'I hate to bother you so much——' she began. But he assured her it was no bother at all, and, since there seemed no alternative, she watched him go with some relief, feeling glad that her aching ankle would soon have some attention.

He was back with the taxi before she had time to wonder how long he might be, and made remarkably little of carrying her that short distance again.

'I thought it was only in books that men hauled about well-built women with such ease,' she said, as he installed her in the taxi and got in beside her.

'Well, you're not exactly hefty,' he assured her. 'And anyway, it's something of a trick, really. I've had some stage experience, and it's one of the things you learn, you know.'

'Have you?' she glanced at him with interest and would have liked to ask a few more questions, but within the space of a minute or two they were back at her hotel, he had carried her in and set her down in a chair in the foyer, and was looking round for someone to whose care he could consign her.

The head porter came hurrying forward.

'I don't know how to thank you.' For a moment longer Natalie refused to have her attention deflected from her kind rescuer. 'Please will you tell me your name?'

'Oh——' he took the hand she held out to him and looked down at it. Then with a rueful smile he said, 'I hate to tell you, but I'm afraid my name is Laurence Morven.'

'Oh, *no*!' She was quite unable to hide her dismay.

'Does it matter?' He looked amused, but also a little stung.

'I'm—afraid—it does,' she said confusedly. And then, as she saw with horror that the door of the lift was sliding open and that her father was about to emerge—'Go now! Please go—*now*!'

Her tone of dismissal was so final that he dropped the hand he was still holding, shrugged slightly and then turned and went without a backward glance.

She was still finding it difficult to hide her agitation when her father came up to her, full of kind inquiries and concern, as was his wont when anything went seriously wrong. Immediately and effortlessly, he mobilised all the resources of the hotel. And before Natalie had time to consider the full implications of her meeting with Laurence Morven, she had been conveyed to her room, examined by an excellent doctor, and had her injured ankle dressed and braced with such efficiency that there was every likelihood that she would be able to travel home to England the next day as arranged.

'I'm sorry I had no opportunity to thank your kind rescuer,' her father observed. 'It was a pity you didn't at least get his name, my dear.'

'I was a good deal agitated,' Natalie said, hoping that this not very white lie might be forgiven her.

'Well, of course, of course.' Her father actually patted her head, as though she were a very dear child—as basically she was in his sight. Then a maid was summoned and, under Natalie's able direction, she completed the packing.

After that she and her father and Charles had a quiet dinner together in their apartment, and presently Natalie went to bed.

Only then could she give up her thoughts completely to the extraordinary encounter in the park. At first, as she lay there turning over the events in her mind, she found it an almost unbelievable coincidence that Laurence Morven, of all people, should turn up in exactly the town where she and her father should happen to be, and that she should run into him like that.

But then of course, as he himself had said, he had come specifically to hear her father. And, given that basic situation and the relatively small size of the town, she supposed it was something to be thankful for that he had not actually booked in at the same hotel. Natalie shuddered at the thought. At least he was likely to be in the district where the one or two good hotels were situated, and what was more natural than that he should go walking in the small park, just as she had done?

Until she had asked him his name she had so keenly enjoyed their small encounter! Not the accident which had prompted it, of course, but the introduction into her somewhat limited circle of an attractive, totally unknown man not so very many years older than herself. Usually her contacts were confined to people who had a direct bearing on her father and his career—conductors, managers, a few favourite colleagues, agents—even Charles. They were all chosen because they impinged in some way on her father's affairs.

And then, almost for the first time, there had been someone solely interested in *her*. Even gratifyingly concerned about her. Oh, why did he have to turn out to be embarrassingly concerned with the operatic world? Why, at least, could he not have been a baritone or a bass—or even a producer? Though as her father thought poorly of most modern producers (frequently with good reason, one had to admit) perhaps that also would not have been a very happy choice.

For a moment she felt more frustration and resentment than she had ever felt before about her peculiar position. It had been all very well for her mother to be happy as a sort of extension of her father's career. She had married him—by choice—and loved everything about him, faults, weaknesses and all. Whereas Natalie——

'But I do love him! I do!' she thought remorsefully. 'I'd do anything—well, almost anything—to preserve his happiness and wellbeing.' But to be an extension of even the most beloved parent's career is not the natural

22

wish of any high-spirited girl. And Natalie, when she was not busy just being the daughter of Lindley Harding, had a good deal of natural spirit.

'Anyway, I could have *liked* Laurence Morven,' she thought, surprised at her own certainty of that. 'It's almost treachery even to think it, but I—could—have—liked him a lot.'

And on that odd conviction she fell asleep.

The journey home next day was accomplished without any real difficulty. The drive to Frankfurt and the flight to London put little strain on her weakened ankle; and, once they arrived at Heathrow there was her father's chauffeur, Roberts, with the car, to drive them to their charming house in Westminster.

'Very pleasant to be home again,' observed her father, going round lightly touching one or two of his favourite possessions. 'Dear me, why do people *write* so much?' He glanced distastefully at the waiting pile of letters, though he would have been the first to be hurt and put out if his fan mail had dwindled.

'Shall I see to those?' asked Charles, just as though he did not always do just that.

'Please do,' replied his employer, also speaking as though he himself usually shouldered that burden. 'Natalie will attend to the personal ones, no doubt. Except——' he had been riffling through the pile while he talked, because the vein of frank curiosity, which was part of his rather naïve make-up, entirely prevented him from really ignoring anything so thought-provoking as a pile of unopened envelopes.

'Ah! Quentin Bannister's writing, if I'm not mis-

23

taken!' He had a splendid memory for anything that interested him, and an equally splendid forgetfulness for anything that bored him, and Quentin Bannister, that well-known conductor, pianist and man of music, was an old friend of his.

He took his letter to the window and spent what were obviously some enjoyable minutes perusing it. Then without looking up, he said, 'Have I any engagements next week, Charles?'

With a brief glance at a big desk diary Charles was able to inform him that he had a relatively free week ahead of him.

'Good! Then I shall go down to Sussex for a few days. It's too long since Bannister and I had one of our fruitful discussions. Shall you come too, Natalie?'

'Not unless you specially want me. There are several things I'd like to clear up in town.'

'Really?' He was faintly surprised, evidently, that she could have anything much to do outside his own orbit. But he murmured something about 'dentist's appointments and that sort of thing', and Natalie said nothing to undeceive him. For suddenly it had come to her that what she wanted more than anything else was a few days on her own. Not to do anything specific, but just to belong to herself, and in some undefined way take stock of her life.

Later she was to wonder if something outside herself had prompted that unexpected decision, because when she was glancing rapidly through some of the newspapers which had come while they were away, she saw with a shock of startled surprise that Laurence Morven was singing at Covent Garden the following week.

Natalie usually kept track of most things that were happening in the major opera houses and could not imagine how she had missed this piece of information at an earlier stage. Then she saw, in a gossip paragraph on another page, that he was replacing another singer who was indisposed in *Andréa Chénier*—'The rôle in which he made something of a sensation in San Francisco earlier in the year.'

'With Father out of London, I could go,' was her first thought, followed only a moment later by, 'if I wanted to, that is!'

But of course she wanted to! Curiosity alone—combined with other promptings which she did not specify to herself—absolutely dictated that she should go. Besides—she suddenly took refuge in the thought—was it not almost her duty to go and hear for herself if this new upstart tenor could in any way, absurd though that idea might be, threaten her father's position?

'Father himself wouldn't want me to go, of course,' she thought. 'He'd regard it either as vulgar curiosity or—or a sort of treachery. But he need never know. And it might be very useful at some time or another that *one* of us should have first-hand knowledge of what he's really like.'

From that point it was not difficult to convince herself that she was pursuing her father's best interests in going to a ticket agency—in preference to the Opera House box office where she might well be recognised—and buying a ticket for *Andréa Chénier* on the night of Laurence Morven's proposed London debut.

25

During the following week Natalie never once heard her father refer again to the casting of Beverley Caine's new opera, but she found the score open on the piano, when she came in one afternoon, and she could not doubt that the subject still caused him the bitterest disappointment and affront.

He seemed in good spirits, however, when he was ready to depart to Sussex on the Monday morning, and even at the last minute, he said to Natalie, 'You're sure you won't come too? The Bannisters would be happy to see you, even unexpectedly.'

'No, thank you—really. I'll quite enjoy a few days on my own.'

'I can't imagine what you'll do with yourself,' he replied in all sincerity. 'Funny, secretive girl you are sometimes, aren't you?' And he kissed her with real affection, which made Natalie feel quite ridiculously deceitful.

The sensation lingered with her until she heard the car drive away, at which point she saw her reaction for the absurd thing it was. What could be more harmless than for a girl to enjoy a few days on her own, even if it did involve going to the opera on Thursday in circumstances of slightly unnatural secrecy?

Even to Charles she said nothing of her intention, although on the Wednesday morning he mentioned Laurence Morven's coming debut and showed her a photograph of him at the dress rehearsal of *Andréa Chénier*.

'Rather a fine figure of a man, isn't he?' observed Charles judicially. 'Quite a good mixture of the poet and the patriot. I wonder which line he takes, vocally speaking.'

'Perhaps he combines them in his singing too,' Natalie suggested.

'No one ever does,' replied Charles knowledgeably. 'If the voice is beguiling and lyrical, he'll go all out for the poetic side; if it's heroic and has got a touch of real metal, he'll be the patriot. That's why every tenor loves the part. That—and the fact that no costumes are more becoming than those of the French Revolution period. I almost wish I were going, but I've promised to take my sister and her husband to the theatre tomorrow evening.'

Natalie said she hoped he would enjoy the theatre, but added nothing about her own plans for Thursday evening. Instead, as her ankle was now almost fully recovered, she took herself off to do some enjoyable window-shopping, hardly admitting even to herself that in fact she was going to look for a special dress for a special occasion.

It must be slightly less formal and glamorous than the dresses her father liked her to wear when she attended a performance as his daughter. Something that would not look out of place in the inconspicuous seat she had obtained, well out of range of observation by anyone she knew in the operatic world.

She found exactly what she wanted. Very simple, very expensive—but she paid the price without wincing, for she realised that the dress was the exact colour of her eyes and, as the saleswoman said, 'it *did* something for her.'

'It's silly, really,' she told herself on the way home. 'What does it matter how I look, since there isn't going to be anyone there to take note of me?—I hope.'

But even if she is deliberately seeking to be inconspicuous, there is not a girl born who does not feel a slight lift of the heart when she glances into the mirror and sees herself looking quite lovely.

Natalie dressed in good time on the evening of the performance, still telling herself that it wasn't a particularly important occasion. There is always a certain aura of excitement about the advent of a new tenor of good repute, of course; but apart from that, Laurence Morven was of no real interest to her. Almost no interest.

There was the fact that he had made an unfortunate impact on her father's career, it was true. But she was not going to hold that against him. She was neither for him nor against him. He was just a new tenor.

She found her way to her seat without running across anyone she knew, but when she sat down she found to her vague disquiet that the next seat was occupied by someone who was oddly familiar. A woman well past her first youth, but with considerable charm and an air of smiling alertness which was very attractive.

She glanced at Natalie out of long, darkly-lashed grey eyes and said, after a moment, 'I know you, don't I? though I haven't seen you for years. Aren't you Valerie Harding's girl?'

Natalie was so used to being identified as her father's daughter that it gave her a strange but pleasant little shock to be catalogued as her mother's girl.

'My mother was Valerie Harding,' she agreed, her sense of caution giving way to a feeling of pleased warmth. 'But I don't think I remember when—where——'

'No, you wouldn't. You were about fourteen or fifteen at the time, but I remember thinking even then that you were going to be a beauty one day, like your mother. It was some end-of-term affair at your school, and I was there because my daughter——'

'You're Wendy Pallerton's mother!' exclaimed Natalie. 'I remember—of course. You were so terribly kind to me.' And it all came back to her in a rush. How her glamorous parents had made the briefest of gracious appearances, totally eclipsing every other parent—not to mention their own inconspicuous daughter—and then departed in a cloud of glory, leaving her feeling that somehow they had hardly noticed her.

'You were disappointed because they had to go early,' Mrs Pallerton recalled tactfully, 'and so you joined up with Wendy and me.'

'It was you who did the joining up,' declared Natalie gratefully. 'I felt a bit like a squashed fly, and you were so kind and made me feel almost important. I wasn't able to thank you then because I was at the almost totally inarticulate stage, but I'd like to thank you now.'

'That's very sweet of you.' Her neighbour patted her arm in a kindly way. 'Is your father coming tonight?'

'Oh—oh, no.'

Her tone must have been somewhat revealing, because the other woman laughed a little and said, 'Well,

29

I suppose one tenor doesn't usually come to hear another.'

'I thought perhaps I'd better come and represent the family,' Natalie stated a trifle disingenuously. 'Anyway, I've never heard him before. Have you?'

'Oh, yes. Quite a number of times,' was the unexpected reply.

'But'—Natalie turned to her companion in surprise—'he hasn't sung here before, has he?'

'No. I heard him in Canada and the States. He happens to be my nephew.'

Fortunately for Natalie, the conductor made his entrance at that moment, and she was spared the necessity of making any reply. But throughout the opening scene of the opera she sat stunned. The evening had suddenly become almost too exciting and disturbing. First the recognition of someone who had been so memorably kind to her, and who recalled her mother so vividly, had greatly moved her; and then the further discovery that she actually formed a further link with Laurence Morven seemed almost uncanny.

'I didn't even ask about Wendy,' she thought in passing. Then Laurence Morven came on to the stage and she forgot altogether about Wendy Pallerton.

Charles had been right about the costumes. They were immensely becoming to most of the people taking part in the elegant eighteenth-century drawing-room scene; and as the new tenor moved easily among the other figures on the stage Natalie thought how well he looked. There was nothing of her father's instant impact, which invariably established him at once as the star of the occasion. On the contrary, he mingled almost unobtrusively with the other guests, as the poet Chénier might have done in real life.

But when he was called on to improvise a poem to music for the entertainment of the company, he moved naturally into the centre of the scene and his opening phrases were thoughtfully and beautifully sung. The poet described how, one day when he was out in the country, he was overwhelmed by the beauty of nature and the scene around him. And then various incidents brought home to him the terrible fact that the utter misery and poverty of the people of the countryside was in sharp and shameful contrast to the beauty of their surroundings.

Here his voice changed subtly, until the whole song became a cry of angry compassion for the wrongs of those who were oppressed by the very people to whom he was singing. He was a poet and revolutionary in one, and Natalie—who had, of course, often heard her father and others sing this famous aria—thought that never before had it seemed such a natural expression of someone carried away by his own pity and anger. She found that she could completely identify herself with the heroine, Maddalena, as she stood there both fascinated and repelled by this handsome rebel, while the scene broke up in angry confusion around him.

It was not, perhaps, one of the greatest voices she had ever heard, but it was singularly beautiful in colour and tone; and, like all truly fine voices, of a unique quality that made it completely memorable. There was an intensely masculine sound about it, with what

Charles had characterised as 'a touch of real metal', but with this went an almost sensuous quality that took one by the throat.

'What a beautiful voice!' Natalie exclaimed as the curtain fell on a storm of applause.

'I think so too—but then of course I'm a bit prejudiced.' Mrs Pallerton smiled, but she looked pleased. 'I know it isn't a great heroic voice, but——'

'It's much more unusual than that!' countered Natalie, carried away by her own enthusiasm. 'Perfect for the part, because it's the voice of a fighter—and a lover too.'

'My dear, how well put!' Mrs Pallerton was obviously charmed. 'You must come round with me afterwards and tell him that yourself.'

'Oh, but I——' began Natalie. And then they were interrupted by a couple who came to speak to Mrs Pallerton, and Natalie was left sitting there on her own, wrestling with the bold, breathtaking question: Why should she *not* go round backstage with Mrs Pallerton and renew her contact with Laurence Morven?

Well, of course she couldn't!—Or could she?

Until that moment it had never occurred to her to do anything but put the little-known Laurence Morven out of her life. As her father's daughter——

But then she wasn't *only* her father's daughter. That conviction had been growing on her during the last few days. She was also Natalie Harding, in her own right. Her father was safely in Sussex, enjoying his visit to the Bannisters, no doubt. If she just went round to congratulate the hero of the evening, who was to know or comment?

Just as the lights dimmed once more, Mrs Pallerton slipped into the seat beside her again and whispered, 'I went round to see Laurence, and I told him about you and our meeting again. And he wants us both to come out to supper afterwards. I said yes. Is that all right?'

All right?—No, of course, it was all wrong!

But it was also the most exciting thing that had happened to Natalie in years.

Throughout the rest of the evening Natalie alternated between decision and indecision. But, in the final prison scene, with its irresistible call to courage and high endeavour, she knew she had made up her mind. What sort of timid mouse would she be if she allowed habit and a sort of inhibited family loyalty to deprive her of a delightful experience?

Mrs Pallerton, who had obviously taken Natalie's acceptance for granted, observed as they joined in the prolonged applause that there was no need for them to hurry, as no doubt a good many people would go round to the artists' dressing-rooms afterwards. Consequently, instead of going through the pass-door and across the stage, they made a leisurely way out into the street and round to the stage door.

Here, as Natalie had expected, a large and excited crowd had already gathered. But with the ease of long practice she led the way through, received a nod of recognition and permission from the stage-door keeper, who naturally knew her, and turned along the well-known corridor which led to the stairs and the dressing-rooms above.

Usually visits backstage held no anxieties for Natalie, but on this occasion she found to her surprise that there was a nervous little pulse fluttering in her throat, as though she were the rawest of admirers approaching a famous artist for the first time.

They had to stand aside at the bottom of the stairs for several early visitors who were now coming down after their brief visits to one or other of the dressing-rooms. One of these knew Natalie slightly and paused for a momentary greeting before he passed on. Then she looked up again and her heart gave a quite sickening little lurch.

Two distinguished-looking elderly gentlemen were descending the stairs. One was Quentin Bannister, and the other was her father.

CHAPTER TWO

IF Natalie could have turned tail at that moment and run away she would probably have done so. But her father had already seen her and, as he came level with her, said,

'Why, Natalie, what brings you here?'

'The same impulse that brought you and Mr Bannister, I expect.' To her surprise, that came out quite lightly and naturally. 'I was frankly curious about the new tenor.'

'We came to hear the soprano,' replied her father coolly, though he must have known better than most that one does not go to *Andréa Chénier* to hear the soprano. 'Bannister is interested in her,' he added.

'Are you, Mr Bannister?' Natalie turned to her father's companion. 'She was very good, I thought.'

Then she introduced Mrs Pallerton—as the mother of an old school-friend and, after the faintest pause, as the aunt of Laurence Morven.

'We're going up to see him,' she added, and hoped there wasn't a note of defiance in that.

'Then you must give him my compliments,' said her father graciously. But it was a graciousness which hardly covered some slight surprise and displeasure. 'As you won't be long,' he continued, 'I'll wait for you. I'm going back home tonight and Bannister is staying at his club. We can give you a lift.'

'No——' Natalie spoke quickly but with unusual authority, 'don't wait, Father. I'm going out to supper afterwards.'

'With whom?' This time the surprise and displeasure were more obvious.

'With Mrs Pallerton—and Laurence Morven,' replied Natalie, and as she said that she had the distinct impression of crossing some important bridge that she could never recross again.

'I think we should go up now.' Mrs Pallerton, who had been exchanging a few conventional remarks with Quentin Bannister, turned back to Natalie at that moment. Natalie steadied her voice sufficiently to say, 'Goodnight, Father. Goodnight, Mr Bannister. Please remember me to Mrs Bannister, won't you?' Then they were mounting the stairs, Natalie aware that her legs felt slightly weak.

'Did your father mind you coming, do you think?' inquired Mrs Pallerton, with the uninhibited frankness of one who had never had to weigh each word and its effect on someone else.

'He was surprised, I suppose,' replied Natalie, who knew he had been thunderstruck. 'He still tends to regard me as a little girl'—it sounded better put that way—'and doesn't quite like me to make arrangements without consulting him. But, as he was out of London and not really expected back until the weekend, I don't think it mattered in this case.'

Mrs Pallerton said no more, as they had now arrived

at the principal tenor's dressing-room. She knocked on the door which was opened a crack by the dresser, who said, 'Just a minute, please. Mr Morven is changing,' and closed it again.

For the short while that they had to wait Natalie stood there in the narrow corridor with her heart pounding. Though whether because of the recent encounter with her father or the coming encounter with Laurence Morven she was not quite sure.

Then they were admitted, and Natalie followed Mrs Pallerton into the familiar room which, until that moment, she had always associated exclusively with her father.

Laurence Morven got up from the dressing-table and came forward. And, although the romantic costume was now gone and he was in conventional white shirt and black trousers, Natalie realised at once that he still retained some indefinable impression of the character he had portrayed throughout the evening. It was nothing to do with his physical appearance—something much more subtle than that—but it gave him a charm and attraction more powerful than anything she had ever encountered before.

He kissed Mrs Pallerton and then turned to Natalie with a rather wicked smile, and said, 'So I'm not permanently off your visiting list?'

'Oh, please——' Natalie coloured. 'I'm sorry about that brush-off in the hotel. But my father was just coming out of the lift and I thought—I thought——'

'It wouldn't do to be found talking to the rival tenor?'

'Something like that. I know it sounds silly, but——' again she broke off.

'Well, it does rather,' he agreed, turning away to pick up his watch from the dressing-table and fasten it on his wrist. But then he glanced up again with that smile and asked, 'What's Father going to say when he hears you've been out to supper with me?'

'He knows about it already,' put in Mrs Pallerton. 'We met him on the stairs, with his friend Quentin Bannister.'

'He asked me to give you his—his compliments,' Natalie said quickly.

'But didn't feel like giving them in person?'

'I'm afraid not. I'm sorry, that's just the way it is. Please don't be cross about it.'

'I'm not cross.' To her astonishment, he touched her cheek lightly with the back of his fingers. And because there was unusual gentleness as well as amusement in the gesture she felt strangely moved as well as startled.

Then he reached for his coat and said, 'Let's go, shall we?'

So they went. Retracing their steps down the stairs, along the corridor and out into the street, where an even bigger crowd was now waiting to salute the hero of the evening.

As he stood there signing the inevitable programmes that were thrust into his hand, Natalie withdrew a little to one side with Mrs Pallerton and watched, a faint, irrepressible quiver of dismay making her draw her wrap more closely round her. The scene so nearly duplicated those many other times when she had stood in that same doorway and watched another figure smilingly accept the adulation, the outstretched programmes, the particular brand of incense which is burnt at the altar of a successful tenor. And she was looking very serious as Laurence Morven finally gathered her and Mrs Pallerton into his orbit again and ushered them into the waiting car.

He took the wheel himself—a thing her father would never have done just after a performance, being of the opinion that the transfer from the stage world to the world of real life required a little time before one's reflexes were normal. Natalie glanced at her companion's strong hands on the wheel and wondered if he would have regarded her father's theory as affected and silly. She supposed he would, and gave a small involuntary sigh.

'Yes?' he said at that moment, and he glanced at her and smiled as he stopped the car at some traffic lights.

'Why do you say that?' She smiled too, but a little uncertainly.

'I wondered—why the serious expression and the slight sigh?'

'Oh—it was nothing, really.' And then she added, because she was genuinely curious. 'Do you always drive your car yourself after a performance?'

'Usually—yes. Why not? I'm feeling on top of the world tonight.'

'I'm sure you are!' Natalie's tone was warmly congratulatory, 'and with every reason. I was just thinking that—that my father never does. Drive the car himself after a performance, I mean.'

'Well, he's a much older man than I am,' replied Laurence Morven. And, although that was the literal truth and he said it quite inoffensively, Natalie immediately felt defensive on her father's behalf.

'I don't know that he ever did, even in earlier days,' she said stiffly.

'He did, you know.' Mrs Pallerton spoke unexpectedly from the back seat. 'Oddly enough, I was thinking of one occasion—oh, years ago, when you were probably away at school. He came out of that stage-door after a stunning performance of *Don Carlos*, and I was standing in the crowd in those days. Your mother was already waiting in the car. And when he had dealt with the fans and the autograph-hunters he got in beside her and—I've always remembered it—as she moved over to make room for him at the wheel, he leaned over and kissed her, quite unselfconsciously, as though none of us were there. Then he drove off with her beside him, and I've never seen anyone look handsomer or happier than they did.'

'Oh—thank you——' said Natalie, and that was all she could manage, because that sudden glimpse of the long-gone, glorious past brought the tears to her eyes, and two of them actually trickled down her cheeks.

'Don't cry, darling.' Incredibly, Laurence Morven used the endearment as though he had known her for years. 'I know it's part of the past, but no one can ever really take those moments away, you know.'

'I know—I know.' She hastily wiped her cheeks with the back of her hand. 'I'm being emotional and silly tonight.'

'I wouldn't call it that.' He smiled ahead down the road in front, and taking one hand from the wheel he gave her a large, serviceable white handkerchief, which she accepted with a shaky little laugh, and somehow felt much better.

The restaurant where they went was small and quiet, but the Italian proprietor apparently already knew about the evening's performance, because he hastened to congratulate Laurence on his success.

'How do you know I wasn't a thumping failure?' countered Laurence amusedly.

'First because you are the stuff of which success is made, Signor Morven,' replied the Italian promptly, 'and secondly, my cousin, who was there, has just telephoned to tell me that it was the best performance of *Andréa Chénier* since Lindley Harding was in his prime.'

'Hm—thank you.' Laurence then addressed himself to the menu and wine list, while Natalie surreptitiously stole another glance at him and thought, ' "The stuff of which success is made". That exactly describes him, of course. Perhaps that's why I'm a little—afraid of him.'

Conversation flowed very easily during the meal, which was more than Natalie had dared to hope. She had supposed there might well be awkward moments to circumvent, occasions when loyalty to her father would force her to take issue with him. But though they talked about the performance in detail, it was all quite amicable.

Then Mrs Pallerton told him how Natalie had described his voice as the voice of a fighter—and a lover too. And he said that was extraordinarily nice of her, but added, rather teasingly, that he hoped the remark was original and not something she had heard someone else say about her father's voice.

'Of course I never heard anyone say it about Father,' she retorted indignantly. 'It wouldn't be true anyway,' she added simply.

'No?' He narrowed those bright eyes quizzically. 'I thought your father had all the vocal perfections.'

'In his own individual way, he has,' she replied steadily, 'but it's an entirely different way from yours. His voice is actually more beautiful than yours, if you don't mind my saying so——'

'I don't mind your saying so,' he interjected amusedly.

'—and he has more star quality than anyone else I've ever known. But——'

'Oh—star quality.' He smiled a little indulgently, she thought. 'Isn't that a trifle outmoded?'

'Oh, no,' murmured Mrs Pallerton.

And, 'Certainly not!' retorted Natalie scornfully. 'In a mediocre world it's becoming rarer, if you like. But the genuine article is instantly recognisable by sophisticated and naïve alike, and invariably transports an audience. You can't define it and you can't teach it; it's just *there*. That's what my father has, and it's quite independent of youth or age, too,' she ended defiantly.

'Dear Natalie,' he said amusedly, 'when I'm getting on for—fifty-four, isn't it?—I hope there'll be someone to speak up for me as enthusiastically as that.'

'There probably will be,' said Natalie slowly. 'That

42

man was quite right. You're the stuff of which success is made.'

'Even without lashings of star quality?' he countered with a challenging smile.

'You have a touch of it,' she replied soberly, 'and a great deal else besides.'

'Well, that seems to leave the honours even,' he said as he paid the bill and they rose to go.

He insisted on their driving her home, though she wanted to take a taxi, having some vague feeling that she preferred him not to see where she—and her father —lived. As they said goodnight Mrs Pallerton kissed her 'for old times' sake' as she said, and then, to Natalie's startled but pleased surprise, Laurence Morven also touched her cheek with smiling lips—'for the sake of a welcome truce', as he put it.

She thought, as she went into the house, that this was not at all how she had intended the evening to end. But then nothing had really been as she intended on this strange and—yes, magical—evening. And again she had that odd feeling that she had taken a step which could never be retraced.

Natalie was not entirely surprised to find that her father was still up—like most stage people, he tended to keep late hours. And when she saw that there was a light on in the drawing-room she went in resolutely, to find him sitting there, apparently completely relaxed and studying a score.

He looked up immediately and, as she came forward not knowing at all what she was going to say, he observed, 'That's a very becoming dress, my dear. I don't seem to have seen it before.'

'No—it's new,' she said a little breathlessly.

'For a special occasion?' he suggested. But he smiled at her—that entirely charming smile—and she felt as though her whole heart went out to him.

'Oh, Father'—she ran across and knelt down by his chair—'you didn't *mind* my going to hear Laurence Morven, did you?'

'Mind?—no. I was a little surprised to find you knew him well enough to go out to supper with him. How did you meet him?'

On a diplomatic—or cowardly—impulse, she rejected the idea of owning up to the early encounter in Germany, and enlarged instead on her unexpected meeting with Mrs Pallerton.

'I knew her daughter, Wendy, very well at school, and they were both very kind to me then. I found she was sitting beside me in the Opera House and of course we talked of old times, and I found she was related to Laurence Morven and—and really it was she who arranged the meeting and the supper afterwards.'

'You didn't feel it might have been better to plead a previous engagement?'

'No,' said Natalie, and then found she could add nothing to that.

'You're usually very perceptive over these things,' her father said musingly. 'Didn't it strike you that, as my daughter, you would be better advised not to have any personal involvement with Morven?'

'Yes, I thought of that,' Natalie admitted steadily. 'But, *as myself*, I wanted to accept the invitation. I had

44

enjoyed the performance. I was interested because'—
she hesitated—'he is very good, isn't he?'

'Frighteningly good,' was the strange thing her father
said. And in confusion and dismay Natalie dropped
her glance to the book that was still on his knee, and
saw that it was the score of the new Beverley Caine
opera.

'I see why he got the part,' said her father, and closed
the score with a finality that struck her to the heart.

'He can't *compare* with you in most ways!' she cried,
in a sudden access of anguished love and loyalty.

'Did you tell him that?' asked her father rather
amusedly, and he lightly touched her hair.

'I told him your voice was more beautiful than his,
and then we spoke of star quality—and I said he had
a touch of it, but that you had more of it than anyone
else I'd ever known or seen.'

'Dear me! How did he take that?'

'Quite well,' Natalie recalled with some surprise.

'Then he must be either cleverer or more susceptible
than I had supposed. Did he bring you home?'

'Yes, he did.'

'And kiss you goodnight?'

She longed to deny that, but the deep flush which
spread right to the line of her bright hair made denial
useless.

'Well, I see he did.' There was a touch of grimness
in the amusement now. 'Don't take him too seriously,
my dear. We tenors are a philandering lot, on the
whole.'

'You weren't!' she countered quickly.

'How do you know?' asked her father amusedly.

'Because you so patently adored Mother. Mrs Pallerton was recalling something she said she would never forget. How you joined Mother in the car outside the stage door one night after a stunning *Don Carlos*, and how you kissed her in front of everyone, just as though you simply couldn't help it.'

'I probably couldn't,' said her father with a slight laugh. 'She was the most eminently kissable woman I ever knew. But you have a little of that quality too, Natalie. Don't encourage Laurence Morven. There's no harm done if it goes no further than supper this evening. Now go along to bed.'

So she kissed him and went to bed, aware that she had got off much more lightly than she could have expected. In another mood her father would have been quite capable of staging a splendid scene of paternal reproach, but tonight he had been strangely indulgent and almost understanding. Perhaps he himself had not been quite indifferent to the charm and talent of the new tenor; perhaps the reference to her mother had had its softening effect. Perhaps, even, he was beginning to realise that his daughter was entitled to a life of her own.

And then she recalled, with a sharp sense of wariness, the note on which the scene had ended.

'Don't encourage Laurence Morven,' he had said. 'There's no harm done if it goes no further than supper this evening.'

Suddenly she knew that there was the crux of the matter. He was not grudging her her little romantic flutter, since what was done was done. But, if she understood him aright, it was not to go any further.

She told herself that in all probability there was no question of the association going any further. Laurence had said nothing about any further meeting. But he had kissed her goodnight. Odd that her father had even guessed that . . .

And on that thought she fell asleep.

The reviews next morning ranged from good to ecstatic, and Natalie read them all. Even the one which inevitably—and fatuously—hailed Laurence Morven as 'the new Lindley Harding'.

'Strange how the truly ignorant always feel impelled to make totally inaccurate comparisons,' observed Charles, looking up from this particular newspaper. 'Just as every piping little soprano with a dash of Greek in her background is automatically referred to as "the new Callas". I imagine Morven and your father are about as different as two good tenors can be.'

'Broadly speaking—yes,' said Natalie. 'He's awfully good, Charles. I went to hear him last night.'

'You did?' Her father's secretary looked up in surprise. 'On the spur of the moment?—just like that?'

'No, rather deliberately, to tell the truth. But Father did too, you know. That's why he came back to London a day early. He and Quentin Bannister went—ostensibly to hear the soprano. We met backstage.'

'That must have provided something of a tableau!'

'Well, it did rather. But he took it quite well in the end.'

'Perhaps they really *had* come to hear the soprano.'

'Nonsense.' Natalie scouted the notion with amused good humour. 'Who goes to hear the Maddalena when a new tenor is making his debut as Andréa?'

'Well, that's true,' Charles laughed. 'Was she good?'

'Very good. Not ideal for Maddalena, I would have said—her voice has a slightly mezzo-ish quality which could be very telling in some more sexy rôle.'

'She's Morven's girl-friend, isn't she?' Charles asked carelessly, and Natalie turned a page of his newspaper before she asked, 'What did you say?'

'That's the backstage gossip, anyway.' Charles always knew all the backstage gossip. 'I suppose he's *got* a girl-friend, good-looking as he is, and they sing together quite a lot, so she's as good a bet as anyone.'

'She didn't go out with him after the performance,' Natalie was surprised to hear herself state with some emphasis.

'No? How do you know?'

'Because I did,' replied Natalie, and went back to her newspaper.

'Say that again,' said Charles, after a moment of stunned silence.

'I went out to supper with Laurence Morven after the performance. And with his aunt,' she added, as an afterthought.

'Good lord! Does he travel around with an aunt for chaperone?'

'Not to my knowledge. I went to school with her daughter, and we found we were sitting side by side at the opera. The rest followed quite naturally.'

'You don't say!' She knew Charles was looking at

her with some curiosity, but she refused to glance up. 'It must have been quite an evening, all told.'

'It was,' said Natalie. And then her father came in, and both Natalie and Charles would have changed the subject if he had not remarked with admirable composure,

'I see Laurence Morven had a very good press. And Minna Kolney too. A very gifted young woman, but not ideally cast for Maddalena.'

'Natalie was saying the same thing,' Charles volunteered with equal composure. 'I understand both you and she were there last night. How did you find the new tenor?'

'Very interesting,' replied Lindley Harding, knowing quite well that that word is the kiss of death when applied either to a new work or a new performer.

'Hm——' said Charles, and left it at that, while Natalie thought of the raw truth with which her father had described Laurence Morven last night as 'frighteningly good'.

The next few days slid by in leisurely uneventfulness, but Natalie was aware of a degree of tension in herself which had little to do with her father or his affairs. It was mostly concerned with the odd way her nerves tautened every time the telephone bell rang.

And then one afternoon, when she was beginning to react more normally to the summons of the telephone, her father lazily answered the call—a chore he usually left to others—and then held out the receiver to her.

'It's for you, Natalie.'

She took the receiver and said in a formal tone, 'This is Natalie Harding.' And Laurence Morven's voice replied, 'Was that your father who answered first?'

'Yes, it was. Who is it, please?' Even to herself she sounded like an amateur actress saying her one line in the play.

'You know darned well who it is,' was the amused reply, 'but I suppose the situation is tricky. Is he still in the room?'

'Yes.' She was so anxious not to be drawn into anything remotely conspiratorial that her tone was curt.

'Oh. Well, let's keep it simple, then. When am I going to see you again?'

'I have no idea,' replied Natalie to this anything but simple question.

'Not so simple as I intended, was it?' He evidently sensed her dilemma. 'We'll make it a "yes" and "no" conversation. Do you *want* to see me again?'

She was so long answering that that he said, 'Are you still there?'

'Yes, I am. But I'm afraid I really can't talk to you now. I—I'm busy.' And, although it wrung her heart to do so, she replaced the receiver.

'If that was Laurence Morven to whom you were talking,' said her father, without even looking up from his book, 'you handled him rather well.'

'Do you think so?' Natalie's voice was almost sulky. Then she went upstairs to her own room and sat on her bed and cried.

'It's all so *silly*!' she told herself. 'Of course I want

to see him, and why the *hell* can't I say so?—just be-cause Father happens to be sitting there. It isn't as though he's a tyrant—at least, not in a beastly way. What must I have sounded like to Laurence? Either a poor, spineless creature or someone determined to give him the brush-off.'

Now, of course, she could think of several brief but clever answers she could have made. Answers which would have conveyed nothing to her father, but would have implied to Laurence that, at a more propitious time, she would be glad to hear from him again.

'It isn't as though I have any idea where I could phone him back,' she thought, chewing a knuckle with vexation. 'If I couldn't have thought of anything clever to say, why didn't I just say, "Yes, I'd love to see you again," make some arrangement and then have it out with Father later?'

But she knew the answer to that. An answer which involved her whole way of life for the last few years.

Presently, when her usual calm had reasserted itself, she went downstairs again and was relieved to find that her father made no further reference to the tele-phone conversation. Instead, he spoke of the orchestral concert that he and she were attending at the Festival Hall that evening.

'It must be almost a year since Warrender's last concert in London,' he observed. 'It will be quite an occasion, no doubt. Why don't you wear that very charming dress you had on the other night? I've seldom seen you in anything that suited you better.'

So she wore the dress she had thought she would for ever associate with Laurence Morven's debut, even though she might never wear it again. And there was no doubt that she and her handsome father made an arresting pair as they entered the hall and made their way up the gangway to their.seats.

Natalie was used to the rustle of interest and excitement which her father's presence invariably evoked, but it never failed to give her a sensation of pleasure and pride. For his part, though he always appeared charmingly unaware of it, she was sure he really enjoyed every moment of it. And why not?

'Good evening, Mr Harding.' An attractive-looking young woman in a gangway seat leaned forward and actually touched Lindley Harding lightly on the arm. 'I did appreciate your coming to see me in my dressing-room the other night.'

'Why—good evening.' Natalie saw her father smile with that endearing courtesy which could cover, equally, real interest or profound indifference. 'It's Miss Kolney, isn't it? I don't think you have met my daughter, Natalie.'

The two girls exchanged a conventional smile and greeting, and then Natalie and her father passed on to their seats.

'I didn't recognise her without her stage make-up,' Natalie said. 'She's very attractive, isn't she?'

'Moderately so,' replied her father with candid exactness, and Natalie glanced again in the direction of the girl about whom Charles had quoted that unwelcome rumour.

'Good-looking,' she thought justly, 'whatever Father says, and—arresting, in some way. Not a friendly face, but very intelligent——' And then her father made some remark and she gathered her wandering thoughts.

There was scarcely an empty seat in the hall by now, and throughout the place ran that subtle current of excitement which distinguishes some performances even before the first chord has been struck.

'There's Anthea Warrender in the end box,' Natalie said to her father.

'Yes, I saw her. And here comes Warrender,' replied her father, as the conductor entered and—rare tribute —the audience rose to their feet to applaud him.

He acknowledged the reception with a slight smile and bow, and then turned immediately to the orchestra. As if in concerted obedience to an authoritative signal, the audience re-seated themselves, and, as they did so, Natalie saw Laurence Morven slip into one of the few empty seats in the hall. The seat beside Minna Kolney.

With a dismay out of all proportion to the occasion, Natalie stared at them with total concentration, so that the opening phrases of the Egmont Overture passed her by as though they were some meaningless jingle. Even at that distance she saw the intimate little smile which the two exchanged, and noted that the girl's hand closed on his and remained there for a moment or two.

'So what?' Natalie asked herself. 'So what?' And somehow that stupid catch-phrase served only to highlight the agitation and discontent which overwhelmed her.

Laurence had asked her if she wanted to see him again, and she had let him think it hardly mattered to her one way or the other. But for that, she told herself, it was she who might have been sitting there beside him now.

In this, of course, she was going too far, for in no circumstances at all could she have left her father to sit alone while she joined Laurence Morven. But Natalie was in no mood to think logically, or even connectedly. All she could do was look down at her hands, which were too tightly clasped on her programme, and try to pretend that she was absorbed in the music.

During the applause which followed the first item she pulled herself together sufficiently to answer her father's approving comments, and then allowed herself to glance once more in the direction of Laurence and his companion. Her beautifully-poised dark head was near his fair one, and they appeared to Natalie to be talking with a smiling intimacy which excluded everyone around them. Most particularly herself.

Then the concert continued and Natalie—again with shamefully little attention for a brilliant performance— was free to pursue her own thoughts and to ask herself what was going to happen in the interval and at the end of the concert. She longed for a sign of recognition from Laurence, if only a glance and a smile which might tell her that they were still friends. But on the other hand, tact demanded that she should keep as much distance as possible between her father and his younger rival, and so——

The problem was solved for her in the interval by

her father saying, 'I think Anthea is signalling to us to come to her box. Let's go before the crowds start streaming out.' And, as the nearest way to Anthea Warrender's box led away from the two seats which had occupied so much of Natalie's attention, any question of an awkward meeting was avoided.

'Come and stay with me for the second part of the concert!' Anthea greeted them both eagerly. 'Lindley' —he had been a senior colleague of hers for some years—'did Oscar manage to contact you yesterday or today? I've come almost straight from London Airport myself, so I've had no time to talk to him.'

'No, we haven't been in touch, though I expect to see him after the concert, of course.'

'Yes—but there won't be much chance for a real talk then.' Anthea bit her lip anxiously and then, with a burst of that almost childlike eagerness which endeared her to so many of her fellow artists, she exclaimed, 'Anyway, it concerns me as much as him. Lindley—*dear* Lindley—there's to be a gala performance of *Otello* in Paris in two months' time. Oscar is to conduct and I'm to sing Desdemona, and we must —we simply must—have the greatest Otello in the world. You *will* do it, won't you?'

'My dear——' Natalie knew from the slight flush which came into her father's cheeks that he was pleased beyond expression. Not since the blow over the casting of the Beverley Caine opera had such balm been offered to his heart and pride. And it was genuine. That was the nicest thing about Anthea Warrender—what she said she meant. To her he was certainly the greatest

Otello in the world, and she wanted him as a child wants the fairy at the top of the Christmas tree. Natalie could have embraced her.

'My dear,' said Lindley Harding again, 'nothing would give me greater pleasure. There's the question of dates of course——'

'Friday, the tenth of June,' Anthea replied instantly, as her husband returned to the conductor's desk. 'And please don't tell Oscar I jumped the gun in this un-professional way, he'd be furious—even with me.'

'I shall know nothing about it at all,' Lindley Harding promised indulgently, 'except that I am free on that date.'

'Oh, good! Natalie, I do love your father,' exclaimed Anthea.

'I'm rather partial to him myself,' replied Natalie gaily. Then she glanced down into the hall again, and as she did so, Laurence Morven looked straight up at the box, saw her and raised his hand in smiling greeting.

'Who is the good-looking man with Minna Kolney?' Anthea asked. 'He's waving to you, Natalie.'

Natalie was almost tempted to say she didn't know, but had a horrid feeling that she would pretty well hear the cock crow if she did anything so mean. As it was, Oscar Warrender saved her, for he raised his baton at that moment, and her father gave her an admonishing little 'Ssh——!'

For the rest of the concert, in spite of problems still unsolved, Natalie felt happy. Her father had once more been preferred before all others for what promised to be a very great occasion—and Laurence Morven had smiled at her. And, what was more, from a safe distance. She need not fear that he would boldly speak to her—as might well have been the case if she and her father had still been sitting downstairs. They would remain in Anthea's box for the rest of the performance, and go with her backstage straight from there. There was even the reassuring fact that Laurence was unknown to the Warrenders—or at least, to Anthea, making it unlikely that they would meet him backstage. The evening, Natalie decided, was a superb one, and she was able to give her full attention to the remainder of the programme.

At the end there were scenes of great enthusiasm, as was usual at a Warrender performance, and Natalie was amused and touched to notice that Anthea applauded her husband as heartily as everyone else.

Then they slowly made their way backstage to the large room which, in contrast to the Opera House, gave ample space for the conductor or principal soloist to receive friends and admirers. There were already many people there, several of whom Natalie and her father knew, and for a few minutes they were separated. Then the crowd parted slightly and, to her dismay, Natalie saw Minna Kolney enter the room, closely followed by Laurence Morven.

Instinctively she glanced round for her father, intending to shepherd him away from the danger area if possible. But he was talking to the conductor at that moment and it was more than Natalie could have contemplated to interrupt them—even if she could have done so to any good effect, which was doubtful.

As she stood there, undecided, Laurence moved swiftly over to her and asked quietly, 'What was the answer to my question this afternoon, when we were interrupted?'

'Wh-which question?'

'You may not remember, but I did ask you if you wanted to see me again, or if——'

'Of course I do!' She also spoke quietly, but there was a breathlessly urgency in her voice which she could not control. 'Only——'

'Never mind about the "only". We did agree that "yes" and "no" would do.'

They had not agreed anything of the kind, of course, it had been his suggestion and she had been in no position to query it. But, as she cast an anxious glance in her father's direction, she saw Warrender make a slight gesture of greeting to Laurence, which was very nearly a summons.

'I think your father and I are about to meet at last,' he said softly and rather mischievously. 'Wish me luck!' And he went forward with that easy sense of confidence which was absolutely characteristic of him.

At the same moment Minna Kolney came up to Natalie and engaged her in conversation, so that Natalie had no means of accompanying Laurence and perhaps helping to smooth over an awkward occasion.

Hiding her impatience, she turned to the other girl and, because she had to say something, she observed at random, 'I didn't realise that Mr Morven knew Sir Oscar so well.'

'He doesn't at the moment—know him well, I mean.

But he's going to know him much better in the future.' She smiled with a faintly possessive air which Natalie found disagreeable. 'Laurence is going to sing Otello under Sir Oscar in Paris in a couple of months' time.'

CHAPTER THREE

NATALIE gave a slight gasp, as though someone had struck her a physical blow. Then she heard her own voice, thin and cold, say, 'I don't think you're quite right about that.'

'No?' The other girl laughed in a not very friendly way. 'What makes you so sure? Are you in Laurence's confidence?'

'Certainly not,' replied Natalie steadily, though the word made her realise how nearly she had betrayed Anthea's confidence. 'But I can't imagine that Sir Oscar would give the rôle of Otello to a young man.'

(At least—surely, surely he wouldn't do so! she thought distractedly.)

'In my view, Sir Oscar would give Laurence almost any rôle after his recent successes,' was Minna Kolney's proud reply. 'And why should one always have to have an old man for Otello?'

Natalie did not even bother to answer that spiteful little dig. Instead she looked across to where her father and Laurence were both talking with Warrender, and tried to read from their expressions if anything vital had been said. But there was nothing to help her. Laurence was laughing at something Warrender was saying, and her father looked relaxed and urbane—

which could mean, equally, that he was hiding either dismay or triumph.

No one, she thought with melancholy pride, could act better than her father, either on or offstage, when it was required of him.

'I'm sorry if I spoke out of turn.' Minna Kolney's voice spoke smoothly beside her again. 'I didn't realise you carried professional rivalry quite so far. I somehow thought you wished Laurence well, even if——'

'Of course I wish him well!' Natalie exclaimed, though at that moment she was in great confusion about *how* she felt towards him. 'There was nothing personal about what I said. I was merely thinking of the way the part of Otello is usually cast.'

And on that she turned away so determinedly that the other girl had no opportunity to say more. At the same time someone else claimed Warrender's attention, and the two tenors exchanged courteous smiles and went their separate ways.

'Are you ready, my dear?' Her father was beside her now. 'I think we might go.'

'Yes, of course.' She bit her lip to think that even now she had made no arrangement for a future meeting with Laurence. But in the circumstances that might be as well. First she must clear up the question of the Paris Otello. If, by some utterly ghastly quirk of fate, Warrender were indeed going to offer the part to Laurence—and Anthea had spoken too soon and too confidently—then the affront to her father would go even deeper than the disappointment over the Beverley Caine opera.

On the way home Natalie was almost totally silent. It was her father who presently said—rather as a headmaster might speak of a promising prefect—'Young Morven seems a pleasant sort of fellow.'

'Yes,' agreed Natalie with some effort, 'I think he is.' Then there was silence again until they had arrived at the house and gone into the pleasant firelit study together.

'Well, Natalie'—her father went over to pour himself a drink—'what's the matter? I see you're worried about something. And when you were talking to that tiresome young woman you looked both shocked and dismayed.'

Wishing, not for the first time, that her father were not sometimes so uncannily observant, Natalie simply countered abruptly with the question, 'Did Sir Oscar say anything about the Paris *Otello*?'

'No.' Her father swirled his drink round reflectively in the glass. 'It wasn't an occasion for discussing such things. Why?'

'Minna Kolney seems to be under the impression that Laurence Morven is going to sing the Paris Otello.'

She had not meant to blurt it out like that, but her father took it splendidly.

'I thought she was rather stupid when I first met her,' he said equably. 'Even she should know one does not give Otello to a juvenile.'

She wanted to say that Laurence Morven was scarcely a juvenile, but her father went on almost without pause, 'Cassio, perhaps. That girl is quite capable of mixing the two rôles.'

'She said Otello,' reiterated Natalie with desperate obstinacy.

'Then she was wrong. I don't know why you even bother to bring the matter under discussion. You heard Anthea ask if I would be free on the date required.'

'I—I know. But she did also say she was jumping the gun and that Sir Oscar would be angry with her if he knew. I was afraid'—she stopped and cleared her throat—'You don't think perhaps she assumed too much and that in fact, on second thoughts, Warrender might have the idea of offering Otello to Laurence Morven?'

'No, I don't.' Her father sounded amused rather than annoyed. 'People have said hard things of Warrender in his time, but so far as I know no one has ever suggested that he is an arrant fool. And only an arrant fool views the part of Otello as suitable for anyone but the most mature of artists.'

It was true, of course. It was heart-warmingly true. But that girl had been so positive. Natalie saw, however, that the argument was leading nowhere and in addition, she longed to be reassured. So she accepted her father's reasurance—for the moment.

But she went to bed sadly worried still, and she lay there and thought, 'Just supposing Laurence did get the part? How could I ever have anything to do with him again? As it is, everything is difficult enough—and I still don't know when I shall see him. I suppose he'll telephone once more, at some entirely unfortunate time.'

It was not Laurence who telephoned the next morning, however, it was Mrs Pallerton. And Natalie herself answered the call.

'My dear, I know this is very short notice,' Mrs Pallerton's pleasant voice said, 'but do you happen to be free this afternoon? Wendy is coming into town quite unexpectedly, and I know she would love to see you. Could you come along to tea?—about three-thirty or four.'

'Oh, I could! and I'd love to,' exclaimed Natalie. She would indeed, she thought, enjoy seeing Wendy after these several years. But even more did she welcome the chance of being somewhere on the rim of Laurence Morven's orbit again. With a perfect excuse too! For nothing could be more harmless than tea with a friend of one's schooldays. Even her father would see no objection to that.

He saw no objection when she told him where she was going. But he did add, 'Is that Laurence Morven's young cousin?'

'Well, yes—I suppose she is.' Natalie had not really worked out that particular relationship. 'At least, her mother is his aunt.'

'That makes them cousins,' said her father, and the dryness of his tone suggested that her reply had been either dim or devious.

'As far as I'm concerned, she's just a good friend from my schooldays,' retorted Natalie, more curtly than she usually spoke. And she went to change into her most becoming dress, though not specially with the good friend from her schooldays in mind.

Mrs Pallerton lived in one of those attractive Chelsea

houses which overlook the river and have not yet been engulfed by the vulgarity of the Kings Road. She welcomed Natalie with genuine pleasure, and five minutes later Wendy breezed in, with so much of the carefree gaiety which had enlivened their schooldays that Natalie felt her own responsibilties and anxieties slide from her.

Over tea there was a great deal of laughter and 'do you remember?' And then Natalie indicated the attractive ring on Wendy's left hand and said, 'Does that mean you're engaged?'

'Oh, yes! I was just going to tell you about him. His name is Peter, and although he has a beard it's a nice well-groomed one. He's an artist. But he actually sells his stuff, which is encouraging. How about you?'

Natalie smiled and shook her head.

'She hasn't time for that sort of thing,' put in Mrs Pallerton with a sympathetic laugh, though there was a touch of seriousness in her expression. 'She is the prop and stay of her famous father.'

'Well, that must be rather fun too, isn't it?' retorted Wendy. 'You must meet all sorts of famous and glamorous people. Do you know Oscar Warrender?'

'Yes. Though not very well.'

' "Not very well" will do,' replied Wendy. 'I think he's still the dishiest thing in the musical world. You've met Laurence, I hear. What do you think of him?'

Natalie was not fully prepared for this frontal attack, but she said with great earnestness that she thought him immensely gifted and had enjoyed his performance very much.

'Oh—his performance, yes.' Wendy was evidently

65

not a passionate devotee of opera. 'I meant—as a person. You and mother went on to supper with him, didn't you?'

'Yes. He was very kind and—and I enjoyed it.' She had a mad impulse to say, 'And he kissed me goodnight, which was the best bit of all,' but restrained herself.

'He's coming this afternoon, isn't he, Mother?' Wendy turned to her mother. 'I haven't seen him for quite an age. Not since he hit the international headlines. How is he taking it?'

'Very well,' said Mrs Pallerton judicially. 'He isn't basically the conceited type, I think.'

'Well, one could excuse him a little conceit after what's happened to him,' Wendy observed. 'London and the promise of that new opera—whatever it is. The Scala and a new production of *Trovatore* specially for him. And what's this mysterious Paris engagement that no one is supposed to talk about?'

'If no one is supposed to talk about it, you'd better not talk,' replied her mother good-humouredly.

'Well, at least I've heard that Warrender is conducting for him. The first time, isn't it?'

But before her mother could answer that—even supposing she had chosen to do so—the front door bell sounded and Mrs Pallerton exclaimed, 'There he is, I think.'

A moment later Laurence Morven came into the room, and it seemed to Natalie that immediately the whole scene took on fresh zest and liveliness. Although her father could be both witty and entertaining, on the whole she lived a rather quiet, measured existence with him. She thought that never before had she encountered people who met and laughed and talked and kissed with quite such natural gaiety and warmth. They all had a sort of spontaneous animation about them which seemed to her to project happiness of a kind she had hardly ever experienced before.

'Dear me, what a good-looking creature you're becoming,' observed Wendy. 'Sucess must suit you.'

'Doesn't it suit us all?' He smiled and turned to greet Natalie. 'Fate—or my aunt—has been kind to us today,' he said.

'What does that cryptic remark mean?' Wendy wanted to know.

'Nothing you would understand,' Laurence assured her. 'How's the bearded swain?'

'Doing splendidly, thank you. And there's no need to be nasty about the beard. As I was telling Natalie, it's a nice, well-groomed beard, not just a cover-up for immaturity or unwashedness or acne.'

'I must remember that,' said her cousin. 'Was that what you were discussing when I came in?'

'No. As a matter of fact,' replied Wendy rather provocatively, 'I was about to commit an indiscretion when you came in, but Mother stopped me.'

'Too bad,' he said lightly. 'Am I not going to hear it, then?'

'It was about your Paris engagement.' Wendy's eyes sparkled inquisitively. 'And I said——'

'Keep it to yourself,' he interrupted sharply. 'Be as indiscreet as you like about yourself or your Peter, but leave my affairs alone.'

'Will you have some tea, Laurence?' asked Mrs Pallerton tactfully. And she adroitly switched the conversation to the plans for Wendy's wedding, which it seemed was to take place in the autumn.

Her daughter accepted the conversational manoeuvre with a good grace, and turning to Natalie said, 'As a matter of fact, I wanted to ask you, Nat—will you be my bridesmaid?'

'Your bridesmaid?' Natalie flushed with pleasure and surprise. 'Why, I'd love to be—of course. But why me? I mean—you haven't seen me for ages and there must be others who——'

'No,' interrupted Wendy firmly. 'I haven't any sisters, as you know, nor even cousins, except this big hulking tenor here. And among my friends—well, frankly, Natalie, you're extremely decorative without being at all my own type, so we wouldn't steal each other's thunder. It was Laurence's idea, actually.'

'*Laurence*'s idea? But you said you hadn't seen him lately.'

'I haven't. Mother was telling him about the wedding arrangements and he said, "Why doesn't Wendy have that charming Harding girl as her bridesmaid?" Didn't you, Larry?'

'Your version of the story will do very well,' replied her cousin, buttering a scone with some deliberation.

'It's—it's terribly kind of you all to draw me into the family circle like this.' Natalie's eyes were shining.

'Not really. We just happen to like you,' Laurence said unexpectedly. And Natalie looked at him, still with those shining eyes and thought, 'Oh, please, please don't let him do the Paris *Otello*! Everything could be so wonderful, if only——'

'Then it's settled,' observed Wendy at that moment. 'I'm so glad! We shall be seeing quite a lot of each other over this I've been down at the country cottage a good deal lately, but now I shall be moving back to town with Mother to make all the wedding preparations, so we can discuss dresses and so on at length. You'll be in London most of the summer, won't you?'

She thought of Paris in June and said, a little uncertainly, 'I—so far as I know, yes. If Father goes abroad I go with him, of course, but there are no long engagements in prospect at the moment.'

'Do you have to go with him wherever he goes?' Wendy asked curiously.

'I *like* to go,' countered Natalie, quickly and a little defensively. And she thought she saw Mrs Pallerton and Laurence exchange a glance.

'Well, I must be off now,' Wendy got up, 'I'm meeting Peter. But I'm glad we've linked up again, Nat—we're going to have fun together over this wedding.'

She spoke as though it were someone else's wedding, but by now Natalie had adjusted again to the fact that Wendy was one of those people who almost invariably speak casually of the things which mean most to them.

When she had gone the other three talked of unimportant things for a few minutes, and then Mrs Pallerton was summoned away to the telephone and—a little breathless at the thought—Natalie found herself alone with Laurence Morven for the first time since the original German encounter.

She wondered if she might venture right away a frank inquiry about Paris. But before she could do so, he said, 'Come out to dinner with me this evening, Natalie. Are you free?'

'I—should have to phone and explain first,' she began, and when he made an impatient movement, she went on hurriedly, 'Anyone would! I went out to tea, having *said* that was what I was going to do and any parent would be a bit anxious if I then stayed out for the rest of the evening. Stop being unreasonable, just because you don't happen to like Father!'

She had not meant to sound so sharp, but he laughed good-humouredly and replied, 'All right, I give you that. Anyway, I don't dislike your father. I think he's a charmer and a very great artist. I just can't adjust to your sort of loving slavery.'

'It isn't that really,' she said in a troubled tone. 'I wish I could explain. I must seem such a rabbit to anyone as independent as you are, but——'

'It never occurred to me to think of you as a rabbit,' he broke in and, naturally, she immediately wondered how he did think of her. 'And though I sound impatient, I'm not really. I suppose I'm just like any other fellow—irritated, though intrigued, that I don't ever seem to have a chance to get to know a girl I like.'

She glanced down at that, but her smile was faintly mischievous as she said, 'You'd be surprised how irritating, though intriguing, it can be never to have a chance to get to know a man you like.'

'Then come out with me this evening.' He leaned forward in his chair and put his hand lightly on hers.

'As soon as my chatty aunt comes off the phone, just telephone home and make any excuse that seems good to you. But please come out with me. I have my car here and we'll drive out somewhere up the river and dine quietly and get to know each other.'

Suddenly the prospect was so breathtakingly wonderful that she was almost frightened to realise how much it meant to her. Without knowing it, she passed the tip of her tongue over suddenly dry lips, like a child who glimpses a treat beyond all expectations.

'I'd love it,' she said huskily.

Then Mrs Pallerton came back into the room, and Natalie realised that she had missed her opportunity to ask outright about Paris. But that hardly mattered now, because she was to have the whole evening with him.

'Please may I use your phone, Mrs Pallerton?' She had no idea that there was an entirely new note of confidence and resolution in her voice. 'Laurence has kindly asked me out to dinner, and I just want them to know at home that I shan't be back until later.'

'Of course, darling!' Mrs Pallerton's tone was more heartily approving than perhaps was strictly necessary. But Natalie didn't notice that. Nor did she know that, as the door closed behind her, Mrs Pallerton said cryptically, 'She said "them" and not "him". Did you notice? It's a sort of step forward.'

In actual fact, Natalie's choice of pronoun was dictated solely by the fact that she instinctively chose to visualise one of the servants, rather than her father, at the end of the wire. It would be so much easier if she did not have to explain—or dissemble—to him.

Her luck was in. It was Charles who answered.

'Charles!' she exclaimed. 'Are you working late?'

'No, I'm just going. Do you want to speak to the boss?'

'Not really—no. Charles, could you just tell him that I'm going to be out to dinner, after all?'

'Just that?' inquired Charles exactly.

'You might add that I shan't be late home.'

'No, I don't think I'll add that. After all, you might want to be late home,' said the understanding Charles. 'Enjoy yourself.' And he rang off.

'It's all right!' She came back into the sitting-room, glowing with happiness in a transparent way that the other two found oddly touching, if she had but known. Then they talked for a few minutes longer before Laurence and she departed, with what could be described as the full approval of Mrs Pallerton.

'It's an open car. Do you mind?' he inquired, as they came out on to the Embankment, where a clear April sunset struck golden reflections from a dozen windows. 'I can put up the hood if you like.'

'No,' said Natalie, taking a scarf from her coat pocket, 'I like it open. I don't often get the chance to feel the wind on my face.'

'Why not?' He looked staggered. 'You speak like a prisoner!'

'Oh, *no*!' She was shocked beyond measure. 'But a singer, you know, has to be careful of such things. And so——'

'I'm a singer too,' he reminded her grimly. 'I hope

72

I never get to the stage of coddling myself to that extent.'

'It's a perfectly ordinary precaution,' she retorted coldly, as she took her seat in the car. 'You might do well to observe it. If you want your voice to last, that is.'

He got in beside her and then said, rather disagreeably, 'Well, do we have the hood up or down?'

'Please yourself.' She looked straight ahead, and wondered miserably what had happened to their lovely, easy relationship.

When he moved his arm, she thought he was going to pull the hood over. But instead he suddenly put his arms round her and his lips were on her cheek, and after a moment he said, 'I'm sorry.' Just that. But it seemed to her that they were the dearest and most significant words anyone had ever spoken to her.

'No—*I'm* sorry,' she whispered, and she turned her head so that their lips met.

'I don't know why I was so cross and unreasonable,' she said, when he released her. 'I'm so happy, really, to come out with you. I just get—prickly, I suppose, whenever there's even implied criticism of Father. It's a habit I've got into—I'll try to get out of it. It isn't his fault. It's just—just——'

'You don't need to explain.' He smiled as he started the car. 'People who—like each other shouldn't have to explain every impulse and reaction. We were both so pleased to be going out like this that we got tense at the very idea of anything spoiling it. That was all.'

It was not exactly a logical explanation, but Natalie

thought it the cleverest and most tolerant explanation anyone had ever offered her. And as they drove on, along the river bank and then by side-roads and unfamiliar turnings until they began to emerge into something more like open country, she felt her whole being relax and expand. And she thought, 'I'll not say one other word that could lead to friction or dispute this evening.'

It was some while before she recollected that, of course, this ruled out the whole subject of the Paris *Otello*.

Oh, but what did it *matter*? The evening—perhaps just this one precious evening out of all the evenings there could ever be—was hers. Hers and his. She wasn't going to spoil it. She wasn't even going to think about the complications of being the daughter of one famous tenor and being terribly attracted by another. If she paid too much attention to that thought it gave an element of something like absurdity to the whole situation. Whereas——

'You're very quiet,' he said at last. 'Is everything all right?'

She wanted to say that never in her life before had everything been more all right. But of course that would be a silly exaggeration. So she just turned her head and smiled at him.

'I'm enjoying it so much that I hardly even thought of talking. Do you want us to talk?'

'Not if you're happy as you are. We'll talk over dinner later. Lean back and relax again. I have the feeling this is what you need.'

'Not really,' she protested. 'I don't live exactly a tiring life, you know. Compared to a great many people I'm almost pampered.'

'Depends what you mean by a tiring life,' he replied. 'No artist is easy to live with, I know that. There are times when I wonder why my family, or my dresser, or my colleagues don't hit me. It's always said in excuse that we live on our nerves—which is true, I suppose. But I have a suspicion that we live on other people's nerves too.'

'You're entitled to,' declared Natalie, happy to find herself discussing artists in general, with no implication that her father was perhaps more difficult than most. 'If you deliver the goods, most of the rest of us are willing to let you have a few indulgences. Did you mean to be a singer from the very beginning, Laurence?'

'From the time I started to grow up, yes. I had a good voice by nature, for which, of course, I can take no special credit. But it did mean that I started with the comfortable idea that it was not going to be such a fearful grind. By the time I realised how much goes into the making of a real artist, I was hooked. And then, as I'm something of a perfectionist in an obstinate sort of way, I couldn't bear to settle for less than reaching for perfection.'

'Which makes it a hard life?' she smiled.

'But an infinitely satisfying one. I've had a good deal of luck as well. There's usually an element of luck mixed in with the hard work, as you probably know. I started with a splendid teacher, for one thing. Then I did have a second string to my bow financially speaking, so I could pay for the length of training I needed without being answerable to some bonehead who was dispensing grants. Finally, although my family thought me slightly crazy, they were willing to let me have my head, especially as I wasn't scrounging on them. It's all immensely important, Natalie.'

'Yes, I know.' She smiled and thought that, so far at any rate, her father would agree with most that he had said.

'In addition,' he added consideringly, 'and with many thanks to the Almighty, I'm almost disgustingly healthy. And perhaps most important of all, I didn't fall in love at the wrong time.'

'What does that mean, exactly?' she asked, amused.

'That although of course there were the usual flirtations and palpitations natural to youth, I never met anyone more important to me than my career. In those vital early years your art has to be your love, if you're aiming for the top. It's easy—and very human, of course—to take your eye off the ball and get deeply involved with things and people who then have a right to first place in your life. But it's bad for art, I'm afraid.' And he laughed.

'You don't think that a rather cold-blooded approach to life?' she said doubtfully.

'No. You ask your father. How old was he when he married your mother?'

She was almost startled into giving an accurate answer, but caught back the revealing words just in time. Instead, she said thoughtfully, 'I suppose you're right. He was a completely established artist by the time he met and married her. And I think he would agree with pretty well everything you've said. There is the same touch of—ruthlessness about him when it comes to his art.'

'No, it's not ruthlessness,' Laurence insisted. 'It's a matter of knowing what you want and being willing to pay the necessary price for it. Anyway, here we are at the restaurant I had in mind. How do you like the look of it?'

She said with truth that she thought it enchanting. And as they went in together to the charming, candlelit place which stood almost at the water's edge, more than one person turned to glance at the happy, handsome pair they made.

Over their meal he made her talk a little more about herself; not the controversial subject of her present life with her father, but more of the days when her mother had been alive, and life had been an alternation of schooldays and the occasional flashes of excitement and glamour when she spent holidays with her parents.

'Whom did you love best in the world then?' he suddenly asked unexpectedly.

'My father,' she said, without hesitation.

'Not your mother?'

'Oh, Mother too—of course. But Father was the dominant figure. He was the pivot of her existence and so, quite naturally, of mine too. And I loved it. Don't think anything else. I enjoyed every new triumph, if I happened to be at home when he took on a new rôle. I'd find it hard to tell you in which rôle he was finest.'

And then suddenly she saw the perfect opportunity for her inquiry and, almost carelessly, she asked, 'What rôle would *you* most like to play, Laurence? I mean—of the rôles you haven't yet played.'

'Oh, my dear'—he laughed protestingly—'how can one say? Something demanding dramatic art as well as purely vocal art. And, by both temperament and quality of voice, I lean more to the French and Italian schools than the German.'

'You're narrowing it down, anyway.' She smiled at him across the table. 'Take it a little further.'

'Well, like old Martinelli, I think I would say, "Verdi is my king—my emperor." And that being so, I suppose I would regard Otello as the crown of my career.'

'Would you?' Natalie spoke a little faintly. 'It—I think it's my father's favourite rôle too.'

'Very likely,' he replied, and then he changed the subject—rather abruptly, it seemed to her.

With a great effort, she followed all he was saying and carried on her part of the conversation very ably. But the magic had gone out of the evening, and she felt as Pandora must have felt when she opened the forbidden box. Unwelcome truth—the certain disturber of her peace—had been liberated.

By the time they started home it was dark, and as they drove along a small crescent moon seemed to drift in and out among scurrying clouds. It was a romantic enough setting, but Natalie felt a band of anxiety tightening round her heart, and the clouds were more significant than the moonlight at that moment.

As they neared home, she drew a quick, irrepressible

sigh, and he flashed a smile at her and asked, 'Wasn't it a good evening after all, Natalie?'

'It was a lovely evening!' She roused herself. 'But'—there was a long pause, which he did not seek to break, and she finally went on—'may I ask something which isn't really my business? Something connected with what Wendy was going to say when you came in this afternoon.'

'If you must.' His voice sounded slightly wary all at once, and she knew that for him too the magic had gone out of the evening.

'Are you going to sing—a new rôle in Paris in June?' Even now, she could not bring herself to name the fatal rôle.

'I am.' There was a note of grim determination in his voice which shook her. But she went on steadily, 'A gala performance under Warrender?'

'A gala performance under Warrender. Any objections?'

'Laurence,' she said, very quickly and breathlessly, 'my father thinks he is going to sing that rôle. It—I don't know what it will do to him if that too goes to a younger man.'

'Your father?' She almost hated him for the incredulous scorn in his voice. 'At his age? Natalie, he's mad even to think of it. He just couldn't sustain it for the evening.'

'Of course he could!' she cried furiously. 'Much, much better than you'll ever do it. How dare you speak of him like that? As though—as though he's finished. You're jealous, that's what you are! Jealous and brash and arrogant.'

'I may be brash and arrogant,' he said very coldly, 'but jealous I am not. I have no need to be, of your father or anyone else. At his age——'

'Stop sneering about his age! as though he's dead but won't lie down.'

'You said it—not I,' was the unforgivable retort he made. And then there was the most terrible and freezing silence.

If they had not turned into her street at that moment she thought she would have hit him and made him stop the car. She would have got out and walked—any distance—to escape from him. As it was, when they stopped outside the house, her rage was so nearly choking her that it was difficult to bring out even the minimum of words required. But rage also sustained her in her misery, so that her profile was proud and cold as she said, without looking at him,

'I must thank you for a very pleasant drive and meal. But I must add that I never want to see you again.'

'Is that your last word on it?' He leaned over and opened the door of the car for her.

'Yes, it is,' Natalie said. And she got out and went into the house without a backward glance.

When she had closed the street door behind her she leaned against it, feeling sick and almost faint with the intensity of her rage and grief. She could almost hear her world falling around her in pieces. Not only because she had quarrelled irretrievably with Laurence—though that in itself had inflicted a wound which was already raw and throbbing—but because she could not bear that anyone, *anyone*, should say such cruel half-truths of her father.

It was true that he was past his first youth, that for the purposes of public information a few years were always taken off his age. It was beyond doubt that certain rôles were not now for him. But he remained the great artist, the finest tenor of them all. The man who could break or rejoice the hearts of his audience almost at will. There was no one like him. No one! And that absurd, arrogant, jealous Laurence Morven had spoken of him as though he were nothing but a worn-out old has-been who simply had not the grace to retire.

She went slowly into the study, the room which more than any other she associated with him, and she crouched down by the dying fire and told herself that she hated Laurence. That it served her right for being in some sort of way disloyal to her father.

She was still crouching there when her father came in, in excellent humour and looking magnificent in an evening cloak that would have made most men look ridiculous.

'Why, Natalie!' he put on the light. 'What are you doing crouching there?'

'I was cold,' she muttered, and got to her feet.

He flung off his cloak with the same gesture he used when divesting himself of a stage costume. Rather the way Sir Walter Raleigh must have flung down his cloak before Queen Elizabeth, she thought with absurd irrelevance.

'I gather it wasn't exactly a successful evening,' he said, not unkindly, and he came and sat down by the fire and efficiently poked it into some sort of blaze.

'No.' Just the monosyllable. Nothing else.

'With Laurence Morven?'

She nodded.

'My dear, I did warn you.' He looked at her, still not unkindly, but with a touch of complacence in his glance which made her exclaim almost savagely,

'At least it enabled me to find out a useful piece of information. He *is* going to sing the Paris Otello.'

The moment she had said it she was sorry, and she put out her hand as though to sustain him against the blow which she herself had given. She need not have bothered, however. He took the hand she put out, and his was strong and warm round her cold fingers.

'Dear child, stop tormenting yourself about that,' he said. '*I* am singing the Paris Otello. I've just been settling the details over dinner with Warrender.'

'You——?' she actually staggered a little. 'But Laurence himself told me——'

'He was just showing off,' cut in her father calmly. 'Deplorable behaviour, of course, but understandable in a young man of his type. He has ideas above his artistic station.'

'He wasn't showing off.' Her voice was high and strained. 'I questioned him and——'

'He said categorically that he was singing Otello?'

'Yes——' Then she stopped suddenly and tried to recall if the word 'Otello' had been used. 'No——' she said huskily.

'Well, which was it?' Her father looked amused.

'He said categorically that he was singing a new rôle

in Paris—at a gala performance—under Warrender.'

'He is—Don José in *Carmen*. Well suited to his age and gifts, I imagine. But now, alas, rather beyond my own particular capabilities.'

CHAPTER FOUR

'IT isn't possible!' Natalie's voice dropped to a tragic whisper and in that moment she was speaking to herself rather than to her father. Then she added bewilderedly, 'Do you mean that there are *two* galas?'

'You could say that. It's more or less a gala week, I believe. In honour of some visiting potentate or statesman or some such.' Evidently potentates and statesmen ranked low in her father's estimation and he had not bothered to inform himself on this point. 'It might seem excessive in some places, but the French have a flair for this sort of thing. They can mount an occasion with magnificence but without vulgarity.'

Natalie was not really listening to what the French could do. She was recalling her own voice telling Laurence that he was brash and jealous, and that she had no wish to see him again.

'But why all the secrecy?' She snatched suddenly at another strand of the tangled story.

'What secrecy?' asked her father. 'If you mean that I carefully preserved the confidence Anthea reposed in me——'

'No, no!' Natalie was almost maddened by his inability to see a situation from any standpoint but his own. '*Laurence* was so secretive too. That was largely why I thought—I feared—he might indeed be getting the role of Otello.'

84

'Well, no doubt like everyone else he was warned not to talk too much before the public announcement was made. It is rather a special occasion, after all, and no one likes these things to go off at half-cock.'

'So it's Don José that he's singing—for the first time.' Again Natalie spoke half to herself.

'Yes, I think we'll let him have that.' Her father laughed genially. 'He'll probably make a very good stab at it. And now you see you can stop worrying.'

'Yes,' said Natalie, and suppressed the hysterical laughter which rose in her throat at that.

She could stop worrying. She had taken her happiness—she knew that now—and broken it in pieces with her own hands. But she could stop worrying.

'And,' added her father, as he stood up and towered over her, 'the day any young man of Laurence Morven's pretensions takes the rôle of Otello from me, I am ready to retire.'

On this fine exit line, he took Natalie by the arm and, affectionately but irresistibly, propelled her towards the door.

'Goodnight, my dear. You look tired. Sleep well, and don't concern yourself with Laurence Morven. I doubt if he's fated to make much impact on either of our lives.'

She went to bed. But an hour later she was still wide awake, retracing the conversation of that evening and trying to see where and how she had jumped to such a tragically false conclusion. It was, she realised now, her own exaggerated fear which had led her to fog the issue. If his answer had meant nothing much to her one way or the other, she could have asked clearly and simply about the casting of Otello, without approaching the subject in such a roundabout way. It was an instinctive anxiety to hold off the final moment of unacceptable truth which had prompted her to use equivocal terms and talk about 'the Paris gala' and 'a new rôle'. As for the apparently clinching detail that Warrender was conducting, no doubt he was conducting both performances.

'Why wasn't Laurence himself more specific?' she thought unhappily.

But really, why should he be? She herself had set him firmly on the wrong line of thought. And she saw now—reluctantly but inescapably—why he had exclaimed in scornful astonishment at the idea of her father expecting to sing the rôle. No one, least of all her father himself, would think of casting him for Don José nowadays.

Nothing excused some of the things Laurence had said, of course, however much they might have been at cross-purposes on the actual rôle involved. For a moment she consoled herself with the belief that for that alone she would never have wished to have anything more to do with him. But it was a hollow argument. If she, in her touchy nervousness, had not confused things, he would never have had occasion to say what he had. The mistake would have been explained, and the evening would have ended happily.

Oh, how happily! There swept over her, like a warm tide, the full recollection of the joy shared in the earlier part of that evening. Why was it that one could

86

never unsay the bitter things, but so easily obliterate the kinder, happier words that had illumined the scenes one treasured? Was *he* remembering any part of that lovely shared experience? or only recalling with scorn and rejection the way they had parted?

Perhaps he too was sorry that it had ended as it had. Suppose, if she telephoned and said she was sorry, might he not listen to her explanation?

No—not on the telephone. It was always difficult to handle an emotional issue on the telephone. If she *saw* him——

But how did one arrange to see someone one had dismissed with insult from one's life? She had no idea where he lived, for one thing—though no doubt she could find that out from Mrs Pallerton. But the very idea of following him up to his hotel or apartment was unthinkable.

Then the Opera House? He must go there for rehearsals and to collect his mail. She could go to the stage door and ask, quite legitimately, if there were any mail for her father. At the same time she could ask casually about rehearsal times for *Kit Marlowe*. She would not actually hang about like some stage-struck fan—even in the dark she blushed at the thought—but there must surely be some way in which she could seem to run across him by chance. And then she would be able to explain about the complete misunderstanding and tell him how truly sorry she was.

Slowly her jangled nerves were quietening a little, and sleep was beginning to assert itself. In that half-conscious state, it seemed to her that she had found the perfect solution. And a moment or two later she was asleep.

Though she slept well, she woke to a sensation of anxiety and depression. And when full recollection swept back upon her, she wondered how she could possibly have supposed she could go to the Opera House and force some opportunity to speak to Laurence. What sort of pride had she got that she could even have entertained the idea?

But pride is a poor comforter when one is wretched and in the wrong. By the middle of the morning she had accepted her tenuous plan, and resolutely she left the house, summoned a taxi and drove to the bottom of Wellington Street. If she walked slowly up towards the Opera House she would give herself a few more minutes in which she might meet him.

Natalie had always had a certain degree of sympathy with the humbler admirers who drifted inconspicuously round the famous artists like her father. (He had too, to tell the truth, for in many ways he was a kindly man.) But never had she imagined herself emulating the rather naïve tactics by which they sought to make some slight contact with their chosen divinity.

How many before her—from the days of Caruso and Melba onwards—must have slowly perambulated up Wellington Street and Bow Street, past the shops and warehouses, hoping for that magic moment when the One who Mattered might appear on the horizon.

No one who mattered appeared on Natalie's horizon, and presently she turned the corner into Floral Street and, still slowly, walked towards the stage door. Once inside there, she asked with an admirable degree of casualness if there was any post for her father. And— reassuring and pride-restoring detail—there was.

She took the two or three envelopes, glanced at them and asked, almost absently, 'Is there any rehearsal on at the moment?'

'Nothing onstage,' was the reply. 'Rehearsal for principals only in the crush bar, for this new opera *Marlowe*.'

She managed to make some intelligent comment on that and then, while she was wondering what else she could ask, the man at the stage-door said, free, gratis and for nothing, 'It'll be over at twelve-thirty, if you're meeting someone.'

'Oh, thank you.' She smiled dazzlingly in her relief and gratitude, glanced at her watch, noting that it was ten minutes past twelve and, murmuring something about having a coffee, she tucked the letters into her handbag and turned away.

Down Bow Street and Wellington Street once more —and then she found a coffee bar and went in. It was already crowded with early lunchers and, by the time she had ordered and received her coffee, she was already anxious about her timing. So she gulped down half of the hot, rather tasteless liquid, paid hastily and went out into the street again.

And now, the crucial few minutes! Her heart seemed to be beating right up in her throat, and had she been climbing Mount Everest she could not have found the slope of the road more breathtaking. For a few useful moments she stood and stared into a shop window, but presently there was no way of pretending, even to herself, that she could simulate further interest in the dusty artificial flowers displayed there.

She walked on, and was almost at the front of the Opera House when he came round the corner.

But he was not alone. Somehow, she had never thought of that possibility. Minna Kolney, radiating smiling energy and a great satisfaction with life, walked beside him. Fortunately for Natalie, she turned her head away at that moment, to summon a cruising taxi on the other side of the road.

But *he* saw her all right. Natalie knew that to the bottom of her soul. He even looked straight at her for a freezing couple of seconds. Then he took Minna possessively by the arm and shepherded her across the road to the waiting taxi. And a moment later they had both entered it and driven off.

Natalie was left standing there, every other emotion crushed and stunned by a sense of humiliation and disappointment like nothing else she had ever known.

Presently she too hailed a passing taxi and was driven home. And all the way she was telling herself that it served her right, it served her right—it served her right! Dignity, pride, even decent self-respect had all been sacrificed. And for what? A glance of scornful rejection which made any further effort at peace-making totally ridiculous.

The following few weeks were very unhappy ones for Natalie, but she believed that she hid that fact from her father. At least she immersed herself once more in his affairs, and tried not to let anything else in her life matter.

There were one or two meetings with Wendy, and Natalie gave an excellent display of intense and pleasurable interest in the plans for the autumn wedding. She discussed Wendy's dress—and, indeed, her own dress —as though these things absorbed her total attention. And even when there was a passing reference to Wendy's famous cousin, she contrived to show the exact degree of interest required. No more and no less.

At one point she did manage to make herself ask—though without showing the apprehension she felt—'Will Laurence be coming to the wedding?'

'I shouldn't think so,' was Wendy's reply. 'I imagine he'll be back in Canada by then, and I could hardly expect him to come back specially for the occasion.'

Yes, of course—he would be going back to Canada some time, and then the Atlantic Ocean would lie between them. Natalie almost wished that were already the case, for the humiliation which dogged her incessantly would somehow be a little less if he were thousands of miles away.

She tried to tell herself that she was no longer interested in anything which happened to him. But after the first night of *Kit Marlowe* she read every newspaper review, and felt an illogical warmth at her heart because they were uniformly good. It was nothing to do with her, of course, but she would have hated it if he had been a failure. So, by the same token, she was entitled to rejoice at his tremendous success.

Both from her own point of view and his, she felt she

could manage to say *something* to her father on this vexed topic. And so she remarked, in as natural a tone as she could produce, 'I see the critics speak well of Laurence Morven's *Kit Marlowe*.'

'Which critics?' inquired her father.

'Well, all of them, really.'

'Hm—not a good sign. There are some critics whose censure is more gratifying than anyone else's praise.'

'For instance?' asked Natalie, curbing her irritation with some difficulty.

Her father named one or two.

'But they've almost invariably praised you,' Natalie reminded him.

'That,' said her father, 'is different.' And she saw that to him it really was.

'Do you want to go and hear this performance?' he inquired after a moment. 'If so——'

'No!' She spoke more emphatically than she would have wished. But her father seemed to find her reply perfectly acceptable, and the subject was dropped. In any case, preparations for the Paris visit were now beginning to take precedence over everything else.

'I'm glad I'm coming,' Charles Drury told her. 'I persuaded your father that it was absolutely vital he should have his secretary with him. It wasn't really, of course, but his Otello is still one of the few great experiences in life, so far as I'm concerned. I wasn't going to miss it for the sake of a few white lies.'

'I'm glad too that you're coming.' Natalie smiled at him almost affectionately, for Charles was always a great support.

'I must confess also to some curiosity to hear Morven's Don José,' he went on. 'It should be quite an occasion if he's as good as I expect.'

'Who is singing Carmen?' she asked. 'Have you heard?'

'Who do you think?' Charles laughed. 'Minna Kolney, of course. She seems to know how to worm her way into most of the casts that include him. But she should be good in the part. She's almost a natural for Carmen—both by nature and art. There was a not dissimilar part in the Beverley Caine work, and she was extraordinarily good.'

'Then you went to *Kit Marlowe*?' said Natalie quickly. 'To the first night?'

'To the first night,' replied Charles, a trifle defiantly, which was rather unnecessary because Natalie asked immediately with some eagerness,

'Tell me, Charles—what was it like?'

'Attractive, quite strong dramatically speaking, and eminently singable—which is, heaven knows, something to be thankful for in these days. But so far as I was concerned, it didn't quite come off.'

'*Didn't* it?' She was astounded and, to her own surprise, not exactly pleased. 'Do you mean that Laurence Morven wasn't as good as they say?'

'Oh, he was good, all right. Sang splendidly and looked and acted well,' Charles admitted. 'But if you want my candid and, believe me, unbiased opinion, Natalie, I think your father would have made much more of it, even at his age.'

'You mean that?' She was divided between pride in

her father and a sort of resentment that anyone could criticise Laurence, even by implication. 'But—why?'

'For one thing, I think the work is no more than good second-rate. The kind of work, in fact, which requires tremendous conviction on the part of the performers, and a sort of dash and panache which you hardly ever find in actors or singers today. Your father has just that quality, to the *n*th degree. Maybe it's a slightly out-moded approach, and without terrific personality it can tumble over into melodrama, but if it comes off it can make a second-rate work seem a stroke of genius.'

'I do love you when you talk of Father like that!' exclaimed Natalie.

'Thanks. It's nice to be loved—if only as a second best,' said Charles with a grin.

'What do you mean by that?' She had turned to go, but switched round again to face him, and her colour rose.

'Nothing much,' he replied lightly, 'but it occurs to me that Laurence Morven has something the rest of us haven't got.'

'Don't be absurd! I can't stand the man, if you really want to know.'

'That's sometimes the way it goes,' Charles agreed equably. But nothing she could say would make him enlarge on that.

The conversation troubled Natalie a little. But she was glad he was coming to Paris with them. He was good for her morale and made her forget—or almost forget—the humiliating hash she had made of her relationship with Laurence.

To her pleasure, they travelled on the same plane as the Warrenders. And while her father and Sir Oscar discussed the coming performance—a little as though neither of them had ever done *Otello* before, and were just making one of the great discoveries of a lifetime—Natalie sat with Anthea Warrender and chatted on a slightly less exalted level.

'I'm looking forward to the performance immensely, of course. I love singing with your father,' Anthea said. 'But I'm determined to take some time off to shop as well—I haven't been to Paris for ages. Come with me to the Florian dress show, Natalie.'

Natalie said she would be delighted to do so, and further was charmed to hear that they were all staying at the same hotel.

Then, as an exciting yet chilling thought struck her, she asked, 'Do you mean that most of the artists are staying there?'

'I think so.'

The name 'Laurence Morven' stuck in her throat and somehow she could not ask specifically if he would be there. But the moment they reached the hotel she caught a glimpse of him at the reception desk, and she turned her back on him and pretended to be occupied with the luggage.

'Don't fuss, my dear. Charles will see after that,' her father said a little impatiently. And when she turned round Laurence had gone.

Even that brief sight of him had been curiously un-nerving, and yet exhilarating. It was useless to tell her-self that he no longer was of the slightest concern to her; she still ached with misery over the rift in their friendship. And she still hoped that somehow she would have a chance to explain about the misunderstanding. If they were actually to be under the same roof—even if it were the sort of roof that covered several hundred people—surely some chance might occur. Even that very first evening, if they dined in the restaurant——

But her father had no intention of dining in the hotel restaurant.

'No, no,' he said, in answer to her casual suggestion. 'I hate these big, impersonal places. We'll go to the Vert Galant, and dine in civilised and pleasant surroundings. It's on the Ile de la Cité, if I remember rightly. But the taxi-driver will know.'

The taxi-driver knew. And, with one glance at Lindley Harding, he volunteered the information that it was a favourite place for gentlemen of the theatre. Natalie saw that her father was not particularly pleased at the prospect of meeting too many other gentlemen of the theatre, but when they reached the place the way he was received, the instinctive awareness that he was Somebody, combined with the faultless food and wines, transformed him into his most urbane and charming self.

Natalie too was happy to sit there in the atmosphere of elegance and repose, while her father discoursed on his own earlier days in Paris. He could be both amusing and interesting about his initial struggles, even when his daughter was his only audience, and Natalie was feeling relaxed and was enjoying herself when something made her glance across at the entrance as a tall, familiar figure came in.

'There's Laurence Morven,' she said, on a note of breathless dismay.

'Another gentleman of the theatre,' observed her father almost genially. Then he looked across at Natalie and asked calmly, 'Why does his presence here trouble you?'

'It doesn't! At least'—she swallowed slightly—'I was terribly rude to him when I thought he was going to sing Otello,' she was horrified to hear herself say. 'It makes me miserable even to see him.'

She had no idea why she had suddenly told her father. He was, she would have thought, the very last person in whom she would have confided her unhappiness. Nor did she know—because her gaze was determinedly fixed on the tablecloth—that he gave her a quick, wholly comprehending glance.

All she knew was that his hand, which had rested on the table during this quick exchange, was raised suddenly in an unmistakable gesture of greeting and summons. And although she said, '*No*, Father!' she knew it was too late.

The next moment she heard her father say, 'My dear fellow! so you have found this charming place, too? It's a little late to ask you to join us for dinner, we are more than halfway through, but do at least sit down and have a drink with us.'

Still she studied the tablecloth, reluctant to see his face when he made whatever cool and courteous excuse he thought proper. But then she was aware that someone had set an extra chair at the table and, with a murmured word of thanks, Laurence was sitting down between her and her father.

She managed to look up then and, since the two men were talking and no one was regarding her with any special attention, she somehow took heart and stole a glance at Laurence. He was looking serious—no question of that—even a trifle wary. But then perhaps he too was wondering what was behind her father's unexpected friendliness.

Presently, of course, he had to turn to her—but only with the conventional inquiry as to whether she had been to this place before.

'No,' said Natalie rather huskily—and then, to her dismay, found she could say no more. She glanced desperately at her father.

'You must excuse my daughter for being somewhat subdued,' she heard him say, with the perfect degree of rueful amusement in his tone. 'I understand she was deplorably rude to you recently and, quite rightly, she is feeling guilty and self-conscious about it.'

'Oh, no! If I remember rightly, we were both rather rude to each other,' exclaimed Laurence, and although he managed to inject just the right amount of rueful amusement into his tone too, she thought she detected a note of something like relief as well.

'It was—a mistake,' she said eagerly. Though she could hardly believe that she was actually making these difficult explanations with her father sitting by.

'What was a mistake?' Nearly all the hardness and wariness had gone out of Laurence's expressive voice now.

'Natalie thought,' explained her father indulgently, 'that you were proposing to sing Otello—a manifest absurdity. While you, I understand, were under the impression that she was telling you I wished to sing Don José—an almost equal absurdity, I regret to say.'

Even then, Natalie could not help noticing that to her father there was no question which was the greater absurdity.

'You *couldn't* have thought me such an ass as to attempt Otello yet!' Laurence turned to her with a transparent surprise which, she felt sure, must almost endear him to her father.

'It was stupid of me, I suppose.' She gave him a small, uncertain smile.

'I must say, my dear Morven, it wasn't specially intelligent of you either to imagine I would still regard Don José as being in my repertoire,' observed her father good-humouredly. 'But perhaps we might accept apologies all round and wish each other well in the rôles which really do belong to us.'

'Indeed, yes!' Laurence was looking at Natalie now with the smile which warmed her heart. 'I'm sorry, Natalie——' and he held out his hand.

'I'm sorry, too.' She put her hand into his, and she wondered if he also was remembering that the last time they said that to each other they had kissed.

He stayed only a few minutes longer with them and then went to his own table. But it seemed to Natalie that in all the world there was no city like Paris, no restaurant like the Vert Galant—and no father like hers.

How had he done it? *Why* had he done it?

Although she often made herself suspend judgment about his attitude towards her, she knew perfectly well that he regarded her—very lovingly, of course—as pretty well his exclusive property. More than once there had been evidence that he did not welcome the idea of any rival in her affections or attentions. If he had chosen to widen the rift between her and Laurence —or at least to leave it unbridged—that would have been quite in keeping with what she would have expected of him. Instead, he had exerted his considerable charm and skill to put things right.

She glanced up and found him watching her with half-smiling, half-concerned attention.

'Why did you do it?' she asked frankly. 'Why did you step in and make things all right for us?'

'My dear child, why should I *not* try to make things all right, as you term it, for my own daughter?'

'But'—she dropped her voice, though unnecessarily —'you don't really like him, do you?'

'I don't have to like him. I wasn't doing it for his sake. It's you I don't like to see looking unhappy. For a fleeting moment'—he frowned suddenly—'you looked like your mother, the only time I quarrelled seriously with her. Ah, well'—he gave a sigh that was almost completely unforced—'I suppose we get more sentimental as we get older.'

'It wasn't being sentimental,' Natalie insisted. 'It was being the best father anyone ever had.' And, in that moment, she meant it.

He laughed at that. But then he said, more seriously,

'You had let the whole thing get out of proportion, my dear. If we hadn't brought the situation back to a normal level you would have regarded a minor upset as a great tragedy, and I'm afraid the young man would have taken on a dangerous degree of importance. He's an attractive fellow, I grant you, but—as I think I said before—we tenors are not to be taken too seriously.'

She wished he wouldn't say that. But as she looked across at him, she suddenly thought with some astonishment, 'There *were* some adventures before Mother came into the picture. And, though it's an odd thing to think of one's own father, he must have been irresistible in his time.'

She did not altogether forget what he had said during the next few days, but, in the relief and happiness of being on good terms with Laurence again, she thought little about it. Once or twice she met Laurence briefly in the hotel, and each time he had a smile and a few friendly words for her, though obviously he was a good deal concerned with the responsibilities of his new and challenging rôle.

Then came the afternoon when Natalie and Anthea were to go to the Florian dress show.

'It's a special mid-season show, with almost theatrical designs, so there should be some good ideas for concert dresses there,' Anthea declared. 'Don't you want to come, Oscar?'

'No, thank you. Dress shows aren't much in my line,' her husband said, 'but enjoy yourself.' He kissed her, which he seldom did in public. 'And buy whatever you fancy,' he added, almost as an afterthought.

'He's really very indulgent to you, in spite of his dictatorial manner, isn't he?' Natalie remarked approvingly as they went off together.

'Oh, yes! I used to be terrified of him when I was a student, and even when I got my first part,' Anthea confessed. 'But I understand him now. And one doesn't get the results he gets by being soft to people.'

'What *was* your first part, Anthea?' Natalie asked with interest.

'Desdemona. That's one reason why I love it so much. I didn't have the support of your father that first time, of course, but I'm so glad he's doing it here.'

'Do you really think he's the best Otello still?' Natalie could not help asking the leading question.

'No doubt of it,' Anthea replied without hesitation. 'It's the incredible brilliance in the voice. If you haven't got vocal brilliance you can leave Otello alone. Size is no substitute. And then the way he acts it! He always has me in tears at the end. I have to shut my eyes tightly so that the tears won't slip under my lashes. It's quite an effort sometimes.'

'Dear Anthea! Tell him some of this, won't you? I think sometimes he "hears Time's wingéd chariot", and even the greatest need reassurance then.'

'I know! and I promise—Here we are. Oh dear, there's Minna Kolney! I know she's very fine on the stage, but she isn't my favourite person.'

'Nor mine,' said Natalie as they got out of the taxi. 'But we needn't sit near her. She looks as though she's waiting for someone.'

In the entrance to the famous dress house Minna

Kolney greeted them pleasantly enough.

'Have you come after concert dresses too?' asked Anthea, pleasant in her turn.

'No.' Minna shook her head. Then, after a moment's hesitation she said, 'I've come to look at wedding dress designs.'

'*Have* you?' Anthea managed to look interested rather than startled.

'I wanted Laurence to come too, but I doubt if he will. He told me not to wait for him beyond three o'clock, as he was rehearsing.'

'Men hardly ever will come to this sort of thing,' Anthea declared cheerfully, while Natalie felt a deadly chill begin to creep over her. 'I tried to make Oscar come, but he wouldn't.'

'I know——' Minna nodded with smiling understanding, 'but I thought Laurence might, in the circumstances——' she left the sentence unfinished as she walked to the door to look up and down the street again.

'What do you think she meant by that?' Anthea muttered as she and Natalie mounted the stairs together.

'I don't know,' said Natalie between stiff lips.

'He's too good for her! I should just hate him to marry her.'

'So should I,' agreed Natalie with great composure. But not even to the sympathetic Anthea Warrender could she even begin to say how furiously, desperately, hopelessly she would hate Laurence to marry Minna Kolney.

CHAPTER FIVE

LIKE most Florian dress shows, this one was breath-takingly elegant, and if Natalie had been in any mood to think of clothes, she would have hankered after at least half a dozen of the beautiful creations displayed. But from the moment she had heard Minna Kolney mention wedding dresses—with the murmured suggestion that she and Laurence might be mutually interested—she could think of nothing else.

She tried to tell herself that this would not have been the first time Minna had deliberately given inaccurate information or implied something which was only half the truth. But each time she reviewed the few words which had been spoken at the entrance to the salon she found them more disquieting.

A few minutes before the show began Minna had slipped into a seat opposite. (At least Laurence had not accompanied her, which was something!) But then it might well be true that only a rehearsal had kept him away on this particular occasion. Natalie wished now that she—or, better still, Anthea—had asked one or two explicit questions. It would be agony, of course, to know that Laurence thought of marrying Minna; but then it was also agony *not* to know.

After the show, Anthea lingered to examine two or three models, and perforce Natalie stayed with her, to help her decide what she would really like for a concert dress. In the end she chose two, with a cheerful indifference to the price, which marked her as the indulged wife of a very rich husband—quite apart from the fact that she was a highly-paid artist in her own right.

'I noticed Minna didn't stay,' Natalie managed to say carelessly, as she and Anthea relaxed later over tea in a nearby café.

'I noticed too,' Anthea agreed. 'I don't think I altogether believe that broad, but unsupported, hint that Laurence is somewhere in the matrimonial running.'

'Don't you?' Natalie tried not to sound too eager about that. 'Why not, Anthea? She's very attractive, and they often sing together.'

'Lots of stage people are attractive, and *he* doesn't have anything to do with the casting,' retorted Anthea reasonably. 'Of course I think she would very much *like* to corral him, but he——' she paused so long that Natalie could not help prompting her with an anxious, 'What about him?'

'I don't think Minna is his type, somehow,' said Anthea slowly. 'For an odd flirtation, perhaps, but for the real thing——' she paused again, and then smiled as though she had made an amusing and interesting discovery. 'You know, I'd say *you* were more his type.'

Natalie had often thought Anthea Warrender a darling—which she was—but never so much so as at that moment.

'Why me?' she asked, with an admirable assumption of lighthearted amusement.

'There's something warm and genuine about Laurence Morven,' Anthea asserted. 'He's a romantic, and a little naïve—like all romantics. Besides, he's a tenor and, boy! do tenors need a womanly woman to look after them and reassure them that they're perfectly marvellous. Look at your father.'

Figuratively speaking, Natalie looked at her father and said, 'You're not suggesting there's anything alike between them, for heaven's sake?'

'Of course there is.' Anthea was unmoved. 'There's something alike in their basic needs. And you're the kind of girl who supplies those needs. Minna Kolney, on the other hand, just isn't. She's too much wrapped up in herself. Quite legitimately so, since she's a star in her own right, but not the material to soothe tenor egos. I don't mind betting that your father doesn't like her.'

'He doesn't, as a matter of fact,' admitted Natalie, impressed. 'He doesn't even think she's very attractive.'

'Well, there you are! I doubt if Laurence would think her all that attractive either if she weren't clever enough to seem all things to all men for as long as it suits her. Which means, of course,' added Anthea regretfully, 'that she might well get him on a short-term run. Men can be so silly! Except Oscar. He's pretty fly where women are concerned. Though even he once——' she broke off and laughed. 'That was before my time,' she finished succinctly.

Warrender's early flights of fancy were no more than an interesting sideline to Natalie, however. She firmly brought her companion back to the real point at issue.

106

'It would be a terrible pity if Laurence—if anyone so basically nice as he is—should get mixed up with the wrong type of girl,' she said, in what she believed to be a strictly academic tone of voice.

'A terrible pity,' Anthea agreed. 'What about mounting a rescue operation?'

'Whatever do you mean?' Natalie laughed, but there was a nervous little note of excitement in her voice.

'Do you like him?' countered Anthea frankly.

'Well—I do, rather——'

'Then you'd better manage to see a bit more of him,' declared Anthea practically.

'Difficult.' Natalie shook her head. 'With Father, I mean,' she added elliptically.

'There are always ways.' Anthea's beautiful eyes took on a dreamy but innocently calculating expression. 'You ought to come to the *Carmen* dress rehearsal to-morrow, for one thing. No'—as Natalie made as though to interrupt her—'don't tell me your father can't spare you. Of course he can.'

'In actual fact—yes, but he'd simply hate it if I so much as indicated that I wanted to watch his possible successor rehearsing.'

'You won't need to indicate any such thing,' replied Anthea firmly. 'Have you forgotten that I'm singing Micaela? It would be very natural for me to want to have a friend and companion backstage with me, particularly during those long stretches when Carmen has the stage—and José—to herself, drat her! Shall I speak to your father about it?'

'Anthea, you really are the best of friends!' Natalie

laughed breathlessly.

'I don't want to see Minna Kolney get Laurence,' was the simple reply. 'Come on, let's go back to the hotel and find your father.'

So they returned to the hotel together, and the first person they encountered was Laurence Morven.

'How did it happen that you were rehearsing this afternoon?' Anthea wanted to know. 'No one sent out a call for Minna or me?'

'It wasn't a real rehearsal,' he explained, 'just some personal coaching. Where is Minna, by the way? Were you out together?'

'Only in the early part of the afternoon.' Unexpectedly, Natalie found herself able to take a casual part in this conversation. 'We were all at the Florian dress show. She seemed to think you might be coming too.'

'Dress shows aren't much in my line.' He smiled as he used almost the same words as Warrender. 'Did you buy up the place?'

'I ordered two models,' Anthea said.

'And I somehow restrained myself.' Natalie laughed. 'I think Minna did too. She said something about looking at wedding dress designs, which rather intrigued us both.'

It was an effort to say that lightly, but it had disappointingly little effect. He looked faintly surprised, she thought—and hoped. But then he seemed to feel that ended the conversation, because he nodded and passed on, while the two girls went up to the Hardings' apartment.

Here they found Natalie's father rather peevishly

signing letters and photographs which Charles Drury was firmly presenting for his attention.

'How many more?' he asked crossly, as they came in.

'The last three,' Charles assured him, with the cheerful air of a practised nanny dealing with a fractious child. And two minutes later he gathered up the pile and winked slightly at Natalie as he went out of the room.

'Ridiculous, the way complete strangers insist on writing full details of their private lives,' Lindley Harding grumbled. 'Why should I be interested?'

'You know perfectly well you'd be surprised and disappointed if the stream of letters dried up,' Anthea told him cheerfully. And then she went to work with great charm and expertise to persuade him that it would be great kindness on his part if he would spare his daughter on the following day, to act as friend and counsellor during the *Carmen* dress rehearsal, as she would need someone to bolster up her spirits.

'*You* don't need anyone to bolster up your spirits,' he returned with an air of amused indulgence, 'and certainly not for Micaela, which you could do on your pretty head. But why ask me, anyway? Natalie is as free as air to do whatever she likes.'

Fortunately, Anthea realised that he believed he was stating no less than the truth. So she planted a light kiss on his cheek and said, 'You're sweet. But then you always are.'

'Is that the way you manage Warrender?' he inquired with genuine interest.

'No-o. Oscar is harder work,' Anthea conceded.

'Meaning, I suppose, that I am what is nowadays revoltingly called "a soft touch",' returned Lindley Harding, now in an excellent mood. 'Well, go along with you. There's a hint of the hussy about you, for all your innocent expression.'

'I love your father when he uses these period terms,' Anthea confided to Natalie as she went out of the room. 'Who else would use the word "hussy", in that deliciously complimentary sense? Rehearsal's at ten o'clock tomorrow morning, Nat. So meet me downstairs by nine-thirty.'

Promptly at nine-twenty-five next morning, Natalie was down in the hotel foyer, and when Anthea emerged from one of the lifts she was relieved to see that she was unaccompanied. To sustain the rôle of essential companion under the penetrating glance of Warrender would have been difficult, she thought.

'I sent Oscar on ahead,' observed Anthea, as though reading her thoughts. And then, as Laurence Morven came out of another lift and went towards the doorman, she exclaimed, 'Oh, Larry, are they holding that taxi for you? and if so, could you give us a lift, please? Oscar took the car.'

'Why, of course!'

He ushered them both out to the waiting taxi and, when they were installed and it had shot off into the Paris traffic with all the caution of a charging rhinoceros, he looked at Natalie with undisguised pleasure and said, 'So you're coming to the rehearsal, too?'

'She's really keeping me company during the long

110

waits when poor Micaela has to kick her heels backstage,' Anthea explained. 'But of course she must manage to hear and see some of it from the front of the house.'

'I'm glad you'll hear some of it,' he said, 'because I suppose you won't get to the actual performance?'

'I—might. Why not?'

'Your guess is as good as mine,' he returned, but his smile somehow made that inoffensive.

'Well, it depends on—how other things go,' she admitted. 'It's the final rehearsal for *Otello* tomorrow, of course. If everything goes well and Father is pretty relaxed about it, I might be able to go to the *Carmen* performance the next night. But if he's edgy and nervous then I think I should stay with him, in preparation for *his* big night.'

'What it is to be sandwiched between two distinguished tenors!' declared Anthea.

'What about you?' Natalie retorted with a smile. 'You actually have to sing with them both.'

'I have Oscar to protect me,' replied Anthea mischievously. 'Anyway, Micaela isn't a part that carries great responsibilities. And as for Desdemona—well, I'll sing Desdemona any day of the week, for the sheer joy of doing it.'

'Even so, two dress rehearsals and two performances all in four days make up quite an assignment,' said Laurence, as they arrived at the stage door of the Opera House. 'I don't wonder you need Natalie to keep up your morale.'

'I'll send her along to give *your* morale a boost at

some time during the morning,' Anthea promised, 'if you think you might need it, that is.'

'I shall need it,' he replied with a smile. 'See you both later.' And he paused to pay the taxi-driver, while the other two went into the building.

Anthea was sparkling with amusement and satisfaction over the small encounter, until they reached her dressing-room. Then she immediately became the serious artist, with no further thought for off-stage gaiety and nonsense. She allowed Natalie to stay with her until she had completed her make-up and donned her first act costume, and then she said.

'Go round to the front of the house now, dear. I can't even pretend to need you any more, and I like to sit and think myself into the part. Besides, you should see and hear the first act in its entirety. Laurence is really something.'

'I'm sure he is. And—Minna?' asked Natalie.

'You'll see for yourself,' was Anthea's reply. After which Natalie found her way through the maze of corridors backstage and finally into the yawning gulf of the virtually empty auditorium.

Not for the first time, she thought how strange it was that, without the lights and the public and the indefinable glamour of a performance, even the most beautiful opera house looked sad and chill. Even the tuning up of the orchestra lacked the breathless quiver of expectation which exactly the same process could send through the house when an audience was present. In the cold reality of a morning rehearsal it was hard to believe that there could be any magic in store.

Until the conductor came in. From that moment Warrender entered, bade his orchestra a brief, '*Bonjour, messieurs,*' and raised his baton, the spell began to work. It seemed to Natalie that even the temperature rose as the brilliant, evocative strains of the overture seemed to spill out the sunshine of a Spanish street scene, while the darker undertones already suggested the tragedy which was about to be played out.

Anthea's gentle yet resolute Micaela was not new to her, but she found it as moving as ever. The other girl, however, was a complete surprise to her. Offstage, as she knew to her cost, Minna Kolney could be a spiteful and shallow young woman, but as Carmen her impact was stunning. The touch of sultry splendour which was natural to her was perfectly judged and not the least overdone, but what made her performance riveting was the intelligence with which she invested the part, both musically and dramatically. This Carmen was no ordinary sensual gipsy. She was also the brains of the smugglers' gang, and knew what she wanted and how to get it.

As Natalie sat on the edge of her seat, like a child at her first pantomime, the phrase which came to her again and again was the one her father had used of Laurence Morven. Frighteningly good.

Action and reaction are, of course, the stuff of which drama is made, and Natalie was thrilled to find that Laurence was easily Minna's equal. He was singing superbly—all Natalie's experience told her that—and his idea of the unhappy hero was richly individuual. Fascinated—even mesmerised—though he might be

113

by Carmen, he was not to be an easy conquest. And Natalie could already guess that when his final, inevitable disintegration came in the last scene the effect would be catastrophic.

In the second interval she went backstage again to see if Anthea required her, and almost immediately ran into Laurence.

'Larry'—she was not even aware that she had adopted Anthea's easy form of address—'you're absolutely marvellous! Not only the singing. It's a glorious character study. I can't tell you how——' she broke off, too excited and moved to find further words.

'Why, darling girl!' He caught both her hands and drew her quite near. 'Is it really as good as that?'

'Better,' she said, and laughed excitedly. 'I don't know how to say how good it is.'

'And I don't know how to say how much your praise means to me.' They stood smiling at each other wordlessly for a moment, and then he kissed her. 'Come to the performance, Natalie! It will mean a lot to me to have you there. Please come, my dear—and we'll go out together afterwards.'

'We can't. There'll be a celebration supper or something,' she protested.

'All right, then. We'll do something else another time. But please be at the performance—and come on to the celebration afterwards. There'll be a lot of people, but it will be something just to have you among them. Your father could come too, if that would help.'

'He couldn't do that, you know!' She was rather shocked. 'He has *Otello* the next evening.'

'Oh, yes, I forgot the *Otello*,' he said. And even then she wondered how anyone *could* forget *Otello*—with her father in the title rôle. 'Well, then surely he'll need to have a quiet evening, and so you can slip away and enjoy yourself.'

'I can't promise—I really can't promise.' And she pulled her hands away quickly as Minna Kolney came round the corner of the passage and stood still in astonishment.

'Minna'—he seemed unabashed—'it's going splendidly. Natalie has just been telling me so.'

'Was that what she was telling you?' replied Minna drily, and went into her room.

'Oh, dear! Did she mind, do you think?' The words slipped out before Natalie could stop them.

'Mind? Why should she mind?' replied Laurence, and Natalie thought they were the loveliest and most intelligent words she had ever heard.

She went to Anthea's dressing-room then, and offered fresh congratulations. And Anthea nodded and smiled absently, because her big aria came in the next act and she was already thinking ahead to it. So Natalie slipped away without exchanging more than a word or two.

Back in the auditorium, she found there were quite a number of people now scattered about the place, and she heard more than one person commenting on the excellence of the previous act.

'This Canadian is a discovery,' she heard one self-appointed critic say. 'Harding will be hard put to it to make as good an impression when it comes to his even-

115

ing. And *Otello* is a killer if you're not in top form.'

'Have you heard any reports of how he is?' inquired his companion, with more respect than Natalie thought his comments justified.

'Only that he sounded a little tired at one or two of the early rehearsals, but he may have been conserving his strength.'

'Of course that was what he was doing, you stupid, self-satisfied creatures!' thought Natalie, a ripple of angry panic passing over her for a moment. At one time she would not have paid this type of remark the slightest attention. But nowadays it was a little different. *Was* her father sounding faintly tired? Could he still, at his age, completely sustain what had so aptly been characterised as the 'killer' rôle of Otello?

For the first few moments of the next scene she was unable to concentrate on the stage. Then the irresistible attraction of the drama overcame even her own private worries, and once more she became immersed in the work, and in the tragedy which was now rapidly unfolding.

In some strange way, she began to find it difficult to disentangle the stage figures from the people who were performing, and at one point it seemed to her that Minna was indeed Laurence's evil genius, and that they must inevitably destroy each other. By the end, she was almost exhausted, even as a spectator, and when she finally went round to rejoin Anthea she was amazed to find her friend in excellent spirits and cheerfully ready to assess the various high points of the performance.

116

'I know it sounds idiotic,' Natalie said huskily, 'but I find I just can't dissect it like that. I'm still too much under the influence of the whole tragedy.'

'Well, that's fine!' Anthea declared. 'That means it really did make the right impact. Isn't Laurence terrific?'

'Yes. And so is Minna,' Natalie replied, with dogged fairness. 'She—frightens me, Anthea.'

'Me too,' said Anthea cheerfully. 'But then Carmen should frighten one a bit.'

'I didn't mean only in the part. At least, I don't think I did. She casts a sort of spell, doesn't she?' Natalie said slowly.

But then she remembered how Laurence had kissed her and said *Why should Minna mind?* There was something reassuring about that—a reassurance which lasted until she saw Laurence and Minna going off for what was obviously to be a late lunch together. She told herself this was a very natural arrangement, but she went back to the hotel rather soberly, to find that her father had lunched without her.

'I didn't feel like waiting,' he explained, 'especially as I didn't know how long you would be. How did the rehearsal go?'

'Very well,' replied Natalie. 'It made me feel I should like to hear the actual performance.'

'Two *Carmens* in three days, my dear?' Her father yawned slightly. 'I would call that taking rather heavy punishment.'

She wanted to ask if, all the same, she might inflict such punishment upon herself. But she resisted, knowing from long experience that it was better to take each day as it came and act according to the mood—*his* mood—of the moment. It would have been nice to set her own mind at rest, but to press the point now might well provoke a refusal. And a refusal would be hard to withdraw later without a loss of dignity.

The *Otello* rehearsal next day was timed for the afternoon and would, Natalie guessed, probably extend into the evening. Her father had little to say to her on the way there, but she was used to this. She knew that, in spite of the length and distinction of his career, he was always nervous before a performance, and even an important rehearsal could make him tense and difficult.

She remembered her mother saying long ago, 'They're most of them impossible to live with on the day of a performance. One must allow them that.' So she allowed him that.

'You can go straight into the front of the house,' her father told her on arrival. 'I shan't need you.'

Consequently, she was already sitting in her seat when the music of the great opening Storm broke over her head, with the effect of personal involvement which is the acid test of a well-conducted *Otello*. As she finally emerged, feeling battered and breathless, from the ordeal, her father strode on to the stage—a superb figure, with his darkened skin, his remarkable height and presence, and the barbaric splendour of his costume. This was one of the moments one lived for! when that unique, clarion-like voice would ring out in the high phrases of Otello's entrance.

And then no voice came.

She could scarcely believe it. He was, she realised in dismay, simply 'marking', not singing out full voice at all. The gestures, the presentation of the part were all there, but he was saving his voice, presumably with Warrender's permission, and only sketching in the notes.

It was an unusual thing to happen at any final rehearsal; it was unheard-of in the case of her father. She knew he regarded a final rehearsal as being as important and testing as an actual performance. One must be prepared to show one was equal to every demand, he was fond of saying, or admit one was not equal to the part.

After the entrance and then the departure from the stage, Natalie was so shaken that she hardly heard the rest of the scene, even though the Iago was probably the finest baritone in the world. Only when Otello made his appearance once more, to be joined a few minutes later by Anthea as Desdemona, did Natalie come out of a sort of frightened stupor. And even then she was aware of a sense of anxiety and insecurity which she had never before associated with any performance of her father's.

After a few minutes she drew a shuddering little breath of relief. He was singing full voice now, very beautifully and in exquisite harmony with Anthea's silvery tones. To anyone who knew the voice as well as Natalie did, there was a hint of special care at the most testing moments, but with his impeccable technique he negotiated the fiendish difficulties of the love duet, and she told herself she had been tormenting herself for nothing.

In the interval she noticed the critical couple who had annoyed her at the *Carmen* rehearsal, and—despising herself for the impulse—she moved unobtrusively from her seat and slipped into a seat just behind them. They were, of course, already discussing the first scene, with that special know-all phraseology which is calculated to raise the blood pressure of all true music-lovers.

'Never heard him shirk the Entrance before.' The speaker shook his head dolefully.

'Permissible perhaps at a rehearsal,' replied the other, with an air of knowing more than most.

'Well, he can't shirk it at the performance,' was the reply, and they both laughed. Then the first one added, 'He's really over the hill, of course, and probably shouldn't have taken on *Otello* at all. I hope there isn't a fiasco on the night.'

On this the discussion ended and Natalie, resisting with some difficulty a desire to knock their heads together, slipped back to her own seat and tried to still the quaking of her heart. It was absurd, she assured herself, to pay the slightest attention. Fatuities of that sort were the small change of every operatic audience; a mild annoyance to be shaken off with contempt. But she was frightened—really frightened. For, deep down inside her, she knew her father was in some vocal trouble, and only his technique and his sheer grit were going to get him through.

During the next two acts she had her moments of

panic, but she doubted if anyone less experienced than herself would have detected any sign of distress. And there were whole passages that were sung as only he could sing them, while his effortless grip on the actual character was something to marvel at.

Just before the last act someone took the seat beside her and, turning her head, she saw that it was Laurence Morven.

'Have you been in the theatre all this time?' she asked.

'No, I had to miss the first act.' She hoped he also missed her slight gasp of relief. 'I've been at the back for the rest of the time and then suddenly spotted you here. He's everything they say of him—I have an odd feeling that I've never seen or heard the work until now.'

'Thank you.' She touched his hand gratefully and he held her fingers and said, 'Why, how cold you are!'

'I get nervous for him sometimes.' She laughed shakily. 'I don't know why, because he's surefire, of course. I suppose it's natural to be nervous for the people one loves.'

'If you come to hear me tomorrow night, will you be a little nervous for me, Natalie?' He spoke softly and a trifle mischievously. But Warrender came back to the orchestra pit just then, so she just whispered, 'Hush!' Though she left her hand in his.

The last act, of course, was largely Anthea's, and exquisitely she sang the heavenly music which Verdi gave to the doomed Desdemona.

'How unbelievably touching she is,' whispered Natalie, in the silence which succeeded the final notes of the Ave Maria.

'Yes,' he whispered back. 'They say that's the point when Warrender fell in love with her, and I shouldn't wonder if it's true.'

Then came the fateful chords of Otello's entry, and from then until the end of the opera Natalie was aware that her father dominated not only the scene but the fascinated man sitting beside her. He leaned forward, as though to catch every significant gesture—economical though these were—and throughout the great final monologue he held Natalie's hand so tightly that it hurt.

Only Natalie—and probably Warrender too—knew that her father gave the last dying gasps a couple of moments too soon for his usual perfect timing. There was not, Natalie felt frightenedly, a single note left in him.

But Laurence said, 'No one else will ever do it quite like that again. Of that I'm certain.'

She murmured, 'I think so too,' but then added hurriedly, 'I must go. I must see he doesn't tire himself now, but remains fresh for the actual performance.'

'Tell him to rest so thoroughly that he can dispense with you tomorrow night,' Laurence returned lightly. And then he said again, 'It will mean a lot to me, Natalie, if you're there.'

It was true, she told herself, all that was needed was that she should be *there*. She could hardly hope to defeat Minna's wiles unless she was on the spot. She had to be there—with him—making her own impact, so that they could get to know each other in depth, instead of remaining on a charming surface relationship which practically never touched the essentials.

'I'll do my best. I'll do my very best,' she promised, and then she hurried backstage to her father's dressing-room.

She found him looking rather exhausted, as was to be expected after such a gruelling rôle. But he was in good spirits, she thought gratefully, and had the faintly triumphant air of a man who had successfully scaled familiar but always testing heights.

'Was it a shock when I only marked the Entrance?' he asked immediately, but he did not turn from the mirror before which he was removing the last of his make-up.

'A little, perhaps.' She managed to make that sound as though she had hardly thought about it until that moment.

'It was Warrender's idea. I had a little hoarseness in the early part of the day, and he suggested that it would be wiser to avoid any unnecessary vocal strain.'

'Much wiser,' Natalie agreed with emphasis. For at that moment her father met her glance in the mirror, and she saw in his eyes an expression she had never seen before. A shadow of something like fear.

On the way back to the hotel she told him that Laurence had been in the house, and how tremendously impressed he had been.

'Was he there for the first act?' asked her father quickly.

'No. He had to come later,' said Natalie, and she

knew, as if he had actually said the words, that he was relieved.

All the same, he made a good supper and then retired to bed early. Again she had been tempted to tackle the subject of her attending the *Carmen* performance the next evening, but again she desisted, whether from sheer cowardice or innate good judgment she was not quite sure.

'I'll ask him in the morning,' she thought. 'If he has a good night and feels fresh, he'll probably agree to my going. To worry him now would only make him tense and irritable. The morning will be a much better time.'

But the following morning she was hardly dressed before Charles knocked on her door. And when she opened the door he said, with a careful lack of emphasis, 'Could you look in and see your father, Natalie? He seems to want to consult you about something.'

'*Consult* me?' In Natalie's experience, her father seldom consulted anyone or anything but his own wishes, and she found the idea so startling that she went immediately to his room, where she found him sitting in a chair, wrapped in a dressing-gown of characteristic magnificence.

'Is anything wrong, Father?' Suddenly and inexplicably, she was very frightened.

'Yes,' he said, and his voice was undeniably hoarse. 'You had better call Warrender. I have bronchitis and I can't possibly sing Otello tomorrow night.'

CHAPTER SIX

SUPPRESSING an overwhelming sense of panic, lest it should communicate itself to her father, Natalie went forward and put a reassuring arm round him.

'Dear, are you sure it isn't just a temporary hoarseness because you tired yourself yesterday?' Her voice was studiedly calm and reasonable, though her heart was pounding so hard that she thought he must hear it.

'Of course I'm sure.' There was resignation rather than irritability in his tone, and she knew fatally that this was no question of difficult mood or display of temperament. He felt genuinely ill. Besides, he looked it, she thought distractedly. There was a slightly feverish air about him, and a great weariness.

'I'll get Sir Oscar,' she said without further hesitation, and she went across the room to the telephone.

'Just a moment!' Her father's command stopped her in her tracks. 'Natalie, how good is young Morven as Don José? Impersonally speaking, I mean—not just because you're rather dazzled by him.'

'Laurence?' She ignored the reference to her own feelings. 'He's good—very good indeed. He might even be sensational in an actual performance. But, Father, he couldn't possibly sing Otello, if that's what you're thinking.'

'Of course that's not what I'm thinking. I'm not

senile, even if I feel as weak as a cat,' replied her father impatiently. 'But Warrender will have to fill the gap with something, and it will have to be something damned good. If the *Carmen* performance makes, as you suggest, a sensation, he might be able to risk repeating it.'

'I see what you mean.' Slowly Natalie put out her hand to the telephone, and as she did so she wondered how much it must have cost her father to make that suggestion; to be himself the one to offer his younger rival all the kudos which should have been his at the second gala performance. 'You're sure you want to suggest this?' She turned, the receiver in her hand, her finger already poised to dial the required number.

'"Want" is not the expression,' her father replied drily, and then he gave a small but irrepressible cough. 'There are times when one's personal feelings are of no importance.'

She dialled then, and almost immediately Warrender's voice answered.

'Sir Oscar, it's Natalie Harding. I'm sorry to tell you my father isn't at all well. He thinks it may be bronchitis, and if he's right——'

'I realised he was in trouble yesterday,' the conductor's voice broke in. 'I'll come down at once.' And the receiver at the other end was replaced.

'He's coming,' Natalie said. And then, 'Would you like me to see about a doctor right away?'

'Later, later,' her father replied impatiently. 'Warrender will know whom to get. I don't want just anyone playing about with my throat and lungs.' He leaned back wearily in his chair and closed his eyes, so that to Natalie's compassionate glance he looked curiously defenceless; just a tired old man.

Warrender arrived a few minutes later and wasted no time in argument. He knew the signs of real illness too well, and was perfectly aware that no sick man, past his first youth, could attempt Otello in any circumstances.

'I'm sorry,' he said brusquely but with genuine feeling. 'From everyone's point of view, because we were all looking forward to having you the legitimate centre of this performance. But now we must just think what can be done. Any substitute Otello——'

'If you don't mind my saying so, there *is* no substitute for my Otello,' stated Lindley Harding without even opening his eyes.

'I don't mind your saying so, because it's the simple truth,' replied the conductor with a grim smile. 'In which case, we have to change the work.'

'Natalie tells me young Morven may well make a sensation tonight as José.'

'Very possibly, particularly with Minna Kolney as Carmen. Though one can never be certain of these things.'

'We're not dealing with certainties,' said Natalie's father rather disagreeably, 'we're going to have to gamble. *You* are going to have to gamble. Is Morven a good enough proposition to risk a repeat performance? With Minna Kolney, of course,' he added, with a certain amount of tenor indifference towards the name-character of the work.

Warrender was silent for a minute of two, obviously weighing up the situation with the ruthless realism required in such an emergency.

'In default of anything else at this late hour, we can't do other than risk it,' he said finally. 'It will be the chance of a lifetime for young Morven, of course, if he can bring it off.'

'I've thought of that,' replied Lindley Harding drily. And Natalie felt tears prick at the back of her eyes.

'You'd better get him back to bed, Natalie.' The conductor stood up. 'I'll send the Opera House doctor to see him. Look after him well—we shall be needing him for many another performance of *Otello* in the future.'

Warrender was not, Natalie knew all too well, in any sense a sentimental man. But she guessed that was his way of offering a crumb of comfort to an old and valued colleague.

Her father, however, was not in a mood to be comforted. He let Natalie help him back to bed. He accepted the ministrations of the Opera House doctor when he arrived—and the diagnosis that he had a heavy bronchial cold. But then he closed his eyes and said, 'Leave me alone.'

'Is there nothing else I can do for you?' She hung over him, anxious and loving.

'Nothing. I'll ring if I want anything, but I'll probably sleep now.'

Natalie doubted that, but realised he would find any company unacceptable at this moment. So she left him and went in search of Charles, whom she found in the sitting-room of the suite, turning over one or two letters which had come by the morning post.

'You've heard, of course?' She stood in the doorway.

'I ran into Warrender as he was leaving, and he gave me the bare outlines. I take it there's no question of any improvement in time for tomorrow night's performance?'

'Oh, no, he's really quite ill. They propose to do a repeat of the *Carmen* instead.'

'Is he very upset about that?'

'It was his own suggestion.'

'It was?' Charles sucked in his breath slightly. 'He really is a trouper, isn't he? Whatever his little vanities and poses, he genuinely minds more about the performance than himself. No wonder we're fond of him.'

'Thank you, Charles.' She smiled wanly at him. And when he asked if she had had any breakfast in all this upset she looked slightly surprised and said, 'No. And it's a bit late now.'

'Have something sent up to the suite.'

Natalie shook her head. 'I'd better go down to the restaurant instead. Any coming and going will disturb Father.'

So she went downstairs to the almost empty restaurant and ordered coffee and croissants. As she sat there, absently sipping her coffee, she suddenly saw a familiar figure enter and stand looking round.

'Mrs Pallerton!' Natalie jumped to her feet. 'Oh, how glad I am to see you. I didn't know you were coming over for the performance.'

'I didn't know myself if I should be able to, until the

129

last minute,' Mrs Pallerton said, as she kissed Natalie. Then she sat down, ordered coffee for herself and asked, 'How is everything going? I've only just arrived and hesitated to telephone Laurence on the day of his big performance.'

'Then you don't know that there may be *two* big performances for Laurence?' Natalie gave a rather unhappy little laugh and, as Mrs Pallerton looked inquiring, said, 'Father isn't well enough to sing *Otello* tomorrow night, and it's proposed that they should repeat the *Carmen* instead.'

'Oh, my dear, how terribly disappointing for your father!'

Natalie felt almost tearfully grateful that her father's disappointment should be mentioned before Laurence's big chance, and she said generously in return,

'It's a tremendous thing for Laurence, of course. He'll be the hero of the occasion.'

'It isn't so important for him,' was the unexpected reply.

'Oh, it is, you know!' Natalie found herself springing suddenly to Laurence's defence. 'After all, he's the one who has to prove himself. Father's position has been secure for very many years.'

'The young always have time on their side,' replied Mrs Pallerton impatiently. 'When you're climbing the mountain you can afford to slip back an occasional step, but when you're at the summit the slightest touch to your security makes your heart quake.'

'How well you understand!' Natalie's glance was both grateful and curious. 'I would have expected all your sympathy to be for your own nephew and his great chance.'

'I *have* every sympathy for him,' Mrs Pallerton insisted. 'He's a dear boy and wonderfully gifted, and I hope with all my heart that he also will be at the top one day. But if you want my candid opinion, Natalie, there will never be another tenor like your father.'

'You really think so?'

'Of course. It's partly that he was the legendary figure of my operatic youth, and all my generation were a bit in love with him, I suppose.' She laughed reminiscently. 'But it isn't only that. It was his performance I came to hear, quite as much as dear Laurence's.'

' "Dear Laurence's" performance is stunning too,' Natalie assured her. 'But do you mind if I tell my father what you've just said? It lifted my heart to hear you speak so of him, and I think it would cheer him too.'

'It would be more likely to amuse him,' returned Mrs Pallerton realistically. 'I don't think he was in any doubt of the way he was regarded by the girls of my youth. But if you think he'll like to be reminded of it— tell him, by all means. I owe him a great deal more than a cheering laugh for all the joy he gave me. So you've heard Laurence's performance already? The dress rehearsal, I take it?'

'Yes. Both he and Minna Kolney are thrilling. I was hoping to hear the performance too——' suddenly, she was overwhelmed by the frustration and misery of realising there was no question of it now.

'Perhaps there might still be a chance?' Mrs Pallerton glanced at her sympathetically.

'No.' Natalie shook her head, and the tight, aching feeling in her throat was almost more than she could bear. For now, of course, the way would be wide open for Minna. They would share not only one triumph together, but *two*. They would be depending on each other for one of the greatest occasions of their lives. How could that do anything but draw them closer together? And meanwhile she would be hovering in and out of a sickroom where she would not be desperately needed, but where her presence would be—legitimately —expected.

Presently Mrs Pallerton left her to go to her own room, and just as Natalie was deciding she might as well go upstairs herself, Laurence came in with an air of looking for someone, and came straight across to her.

'Drury said I might find you here,' he said. 'Natalie, I'm truly sorry about what's happened, whatever it may mean for me personally. Your father isn't seriously ill, I hope?'

'No, just a heavy bronchial cold, which makes it quite impossible for him to sing. He's in bed now, and will probably have to stay there for some days.'

'Then in that case'—his face brightened, inexcusably she thought—'you'll be able to come tonight?'

It seemed to her, in her anguish and disappointment, that he could hardly have said anything more insensitive.

'Of course I can't come,' she retorted coldly. 'I couldn't leave him at such a time.'

'But you've just said he isn't seriously ill!'

'He doesn't have to be dying, to keep me away from

an operatic performance,' she said almost savagely. 'Good heavens, I've heard enough of them in my life!'

'What about tomorrow night?' He seemed determined to press on her raw nerves. 'He can't be so selfish as to——'

'He is *not* selfish!'

'Well, it seems to me——'

'You do realise you're speaking of the man to whom you owe your big chance, don't you? If he hadn't stepped down——'

'Stepped down!' He flushed and looked more angry than she had ever seen him look. 'No one needs to step down for me.'

'Well, not stepped down exactly.' She hastily corrected her unfortunate misstatement. 'But it was he who had the generosity to suggest the *Carmen* might be repeated.'

'Generosity be damned!' His temper had run away with him now. 'There wasn't another thing Warrender could do, and confoundedly glad he was to have me on the spot, if you want the truth.'

'I don't particularly want your version of the truth,' she replied very coolly. 'But it's nice to know you regard yourself as indispensable. It's always a help when one is —climbing.'

She turned away and would have left him at that, but he caught her by the arm and jerked her round to face him with such force that she actually staggered.

'What did that nasty little crack mean?' he demanded.

'There was no "nasty little"——'

'Oh yes, there was. You were trying to imply that in some way I was climbing on your father's shoulders, weren't you?'

'I was not doing anything of the sort! And let go of my arm.'

'Not until you explain what you said.'

She was frightened then. Not only because he looked rather as he had looked on the stage just before he stabbed Carmen, but even more because she could not imagine how she had got herself into this predicament, and still less how she could get out of it.

'Let me go!' She set her teeth and, when she found she could not wrench herself away, she raised her other hand and gave him a resounding slap on his cheek.

He did let her go then, in sheer astonishment. And at the same time Minna's amused voice said behind them, 'Is Natalie standing in for a last-act rehearsal?'

They turned as one to face her and found her laughing, but in a good-humoured way which seemed to underline Natalie's undignified display of temper.

'Come, Larry,' Minna took him by the arm in a possessive sort of way, 'it's mean to tease her. Both she and her father must be hating you like hell at the moment. But you can afford to be generous.'

He made as though to say something else to Natalie, though whether in anger or conciliation she could not tell, for she had already turned her back on him so that he—and Minna—should not see that her eyes were full of angry, humiliated tears.

After a moment she heard them go away together,

and she was left standing there in the deserted restaurant, her pride in pieces and her world in ruins.

During that day and the next Natalie isolated herself as much as possible from the operatic world and concentrated on nursing her father. But even so she could not avoid some echoes of the sensation which those two performances of *Carmen* evoked. There was no doubt that they had set both Minna Kolney and Laurence Morven well on the way to top stardom, and so remarkable was their achievement that most of the newspapers made no more than a passing reference to the fact that Lindley Harding had been too indisposed to sing Otello.

'Who wants an old tenor when a new one is rising?' Natalie's father said bitterly, and she realised it was the first-time she had heard him apply the word 'old' to himself in anything but the most humorous fashion.

He was not at all easy to deal with during the weeks which followed what he determinedly referred to as 'the Paris fiasco'. Even when he was well enough to travel and they were back again in the familiar comfort of their own home, he remained depressed and unreasonable. Where he had once made almost too light of his age—and certainly lopped a few useful years off it—he now laid gloomy emphasis on it, and tended to see slights where none were intended.

Few of his most intimate friends happened to be available at this time. The Bannisters had gone to the Edinburgh Festival, and the Warrenders had gone almost straight from Paris to the States. As indeed had

Laurence Morven—and, Natalie greatly feared, Minna Kolney too. Any suggestions she offered that they should themselves go on holiday her father dismissed out of hand, saying that he had had enough of being ill in foreign hotels. And when she firmly pointed out that he was now in his usual excellent health, he merely replied that at his age anything could happen.

'You must sometimes want to hit him,' Charles Drury observed one morning, sympathetically.

But Natalie, remembering with humiliation and remorse how she actually *had* hit someone else in anger, hastily declared that this was not her natural reaction.

'I just wish someone would turn up who would direct his thoughts into more pleasing channels, though,' she admitted with a sigh.

And then, that afternoon, someone did turn up. Mrs Pallerton called to consult Natalie about some detail connected with Wendy's approaching wedding, and Natalie insisted on taking her in to see her father.

At first he was in one of his stately moods—the great man in virtual retirement, forgotten by the world. But when Mrs Pallerton began to talk of his earlier triumphs, with a really remarkable degree of detailed recollection, he became more animated than Natalie had seen him since his illness, and capped her stories with one of two of his own which were fresh even to his daughter.

'A very charming woman,' he said afterwards to Natalie. 'Fancy her remembering the dress your mother wore after that *Don Carlos* performance. I'd forgotten it myself until she described it, and then I even remembered going with her to buy it. She had a wonderful clothes sense, your mother.' And though he sighed, he smiled a little too and said, 'Ask Mrs Pallerton again. I like her. Did you say she was Laurence Morven's aunt?'

'Yes—by marriage.'

'Ah, well, I think we might call that extenuating circumstances,' said her father, and she realised it was a long time since he had made that sort of joke.

After that Mrs Pallerton came fairly often, and once she even brought Wendy with her. It was from Wendy that Natalie learned of Laurence's whereabouts, because somehow it was easier to ask her casual questions than to seek information from Mrs Pallerton in front of her father.

'He had some engagements in the States after the Paris affair, I think,' Wendy explained, 'but now he's back home in Canada, having something of a holiday.'

'Any suggestion of further Covent Garden appearances?'

'I don't know about that. But he's coming over for the wedding,' Wendy volunteered absently, with most of her attention on the rival merits of bridal headdresses.

'Is he?' Natalie's tone was so sharp and eager that her companion looked up.

'Yes. Do you mind?'

'Mind? No, of course not. Why should I mind?' Natalie contrived to laugh on a perfectly natural note, though she was in fact bewilderedly trying to decide if she were appalled or enraptured at the thought of seeing him again, and in such intimate circumstances.

'You sounded rather put out, somehow,' Wendy told her. 'And I think Mother had some ideas that you and he had words over the business in Paris.'

'Not at all,' said Natalie, stiffly and untruthfully.

'Oh, well, I suppose it would be natural to feel some sort of resentment,' Wendy observed broad-mindedly. 'It must have been hard on your father to have to cancel, and then see Laurence make such a triumph. I like your father,' she added, inconsequentially. 'He's rather a knockout even now, isn't he? I should think thirty years ago he had lots of girls wanting to throw their caps over the windmill for him—as I'm sure he would express it.'

Natalie laughed, rather glad to have the subject changed from one tenor to the other.

'He was very attractive, according to your mother— and I can well believe it. Though I suppose it's always difficult to view one's father in quite those terms.'

'I don't think so,' Wendy retorted. 'I'm sure my father was attractive enough, judging from photographs. But he was a bit of a bounder too, I believe,' she added cheerfully. 'He died when I was quite young, but I gather that was about the most useful thing he ever did. Mother is discretion itself, of course, and hardly ever mentions him, but I have two gossipy aunts who filled in the gaps very eloquently.'

'Is Laurence on your father's side?' Natalie simply could not help asking.

'Yes, but these things don't necessarily run in families, you know.' Wendy laughed lightheartedly.

138

'Why do you ask? Do you think Laurence has something of a wandering eye?'

'I have no idea. How should I?' Natalie said quickly.

'Well, I suppose since you live in this world you might see something of what goes on.' Wendy turned her attention once more to the more interesting matter of bridal headdresses. 'There was a very glamorous mezzo after him, wasn't there?' she said absently. 'The girl who sang Carmen in those Paris productions. My! that's a rôle to give you opportunities if you have designs on the tenor!'

Natalie found herself completely wordless on this subject, and almost immediately Wendy ran on, 'Speaking of designs, I definitely think this is the one.' And she planted a firm forefinger on the illustration of her choice.

'It would suit you beautifully,' Natalie said with an effort, 'and go marvellously with your dress.'

'And there's no doubt about that being the one for my almost-too-attractive bridesmaid.' Wendy good-humouredly indicated another design. 'That slightly Tudor look requires your heart-shaped type of face. Did I tell you that Laurence may be best man?'

'No! I thought—I thought you said it was to be Peter's brother.'

'It was, but his firm have suddenly offered him a super assignment in South America, and it means his going almost right away. It's too good a chance for him to turn down—the kind of thing he's been hoping for for years. So, when we heard Laurence was coming over for the wedding after all, we thought it would be rather chic to have the family celebrity stand in. Don't you think it's a good idea?'

'Yes,' said Natalie slowly. 'I think it's a wonderful idea.'

'You won't mind being specially nice to him, even if you did have some sort of brush with him in Paris, will you?' Wendy said. 'As the one and only bridesmaid you'll be paired off most of the time with the best man.'

'I shan't mind,' replied Natalie, swallowing hard. 'So long as he doesn't.'

'Why should he mind?' Wendy wanted to know.

'Well—I slapped his face last time we met,' said Natalie with an effort.

'Good for you! I expect he deserved it,' Wendy said in a shamelessly prejudiced manner. 'Lots of men do, and tenors more than most, I should imagine. Anyway, I expect he's forgotten all about it by now.'

'Oh, no, he couldn't do that,' exclaimed Natalie, who felt the occasion was written in letters of fire on her own memory.

'Well then, you must just manage to kiss and make up,' declared Wendy airily. 'There's nothing like a wedding for providing opportunities for kissing. I shouldn't worry about it if I were you, Nat.'

And Natalie saw Wendy really would not, and marvelled at the way some people seemed to sail through life without any emotional complications.

All the same, from that moment her own life seemed to take on a much more peaceful and cheering quality. For one thing, the improvement in her father's spirits made everything so much easier. When she heard him

140

begin regular practice again she knew that time—and Mrs Pallerton—had done their work. He no longer gave his excellent performance of the great artist weary of the world; on the contrary, he went out into society once more and enjoyed himself—for he was a sociable man—and when Dermot Deane telephoned about some dates for the following spring, he not only accepted them, but asked if there were anything of special interest coming up before then.

'Could be,' said his manager cautiously. 'Have you seen Warrender since he came back from the States? —You haven't? Well, I think he has something he wants to discuss with you. I'll leave it to him to explain.'

Later that same afternoon Anthea telephoned and asked both Natalie and her father to dinner.

'How is he, Natalie?' she asked affectionately.

'Absolutely himself again,' Natalie assured her. 'He was a great deal depressed for some weeks after the Paris disappointment, but he's in splendid form now.'

'And vocally?' To Natalie's sensitive ears there was a note of eagerness in the other girl's voice.

'He's been practising regularly for the last two or three weeks, and to me it sounds as fresh and brilliant as ever,' Natalie declared. 'Why, Anthea?'

'I think Oscar has something up his sleeve. We'll tell you when you come,' replied Anthea, and hastily rang off.

Natalie forbore to report these intriguing words to her father, knowing that he set some store by the direct approach where professional matters were concerned. But it was with a lively sense of curiosity that she accompanied him to the Warrenders' famous flat in St James's the following evening.

There were, she noted immediately, no guests other than themselves, so it was to be an intimate occasion, suitable for private discussion. But during dinner conversation was on fairly general topics. It was after dinner that Warrender said, without any preamble,

'How would you feel about singing the postponed *Otello* some time in November?'

'Postponed?' Natalie's father looked slightly startled. 'I wouldn't have called that a postponement. It could hardly have been more thoroughly cancelled—and replaced! Are you saying that Paris wants a performance after all?'

'Not Paris,' replied Warrender, 'here—in Covent Garden. I've been asked to arrange a charity gala, and have been given a virtually free hand with regard to work and cast. It occurred to me that a good many disappointed patrons would be willing to pay very highly to hear the *Otello* they missed in June. Anthea would sing the Desdemona, of course——'

'To make up for *my* disappointment in Paris,' she interjected.

'—and Broncoli will be free to sing the Iago.'

'You mean you had discussions with him before me?' Lindley Harding said quickly, and he frowned slightly.

'Not because I regard Otello as anything but the key rôle,' said Warrender pacifically. 'In fact, without you I shouldn't be prepared to do it at all. We should have to choose something else. But it so happened that some of the important backers for the occasion were in New York when Anthea and I were there, and Broncoli was with us the same evening. It was natural enough to ask if he would be free.'

'I see.' Natalie saw her father smile, and she realised it was the old gay, confident smile which belonged to his heyday. 'It's a wonderful idea, Warrender! The three of us—well, the four of us, of course, including you—just as it was planned for Paris. My dear fellow, I shall be delighted, naturally.'

'I hoped you would.' Warrender smiled too, in a satisfied sort of way. 'One or two of the original small-parters will also be available, I think, and Laurence Morven is to sing Cassio.'

'Laurence Morven!' Natalie felt the temperature fall several degrees. 'Both of us in the same cast? I don't think I should find that very agreeable. Nor do I imagine he would relish the comparatively small rôle of Cassio after his—triumphs in Paris.'

'On the contrary,' replied Warrender imperturbably, 'the suggestion was his. He also was present at the preliminary discussion, and made the offer then and there.'

'Why?' Natalie thought she had never before heard her father's voice so harsh.

'Why?' repeated Warrender, and shrugged. 'He didn't say why. Possibly he wished to make his contribution to a good cause. Or maybe he regards Cassio as an interesting and beautiful rôle—which it is.'

'It was neither of those reasons.' Lindley Harding pushed back his chair and stood up. 'It was his way of challenging me on my own ground. "Let the public hear us both on the same evening and make their choice"—that was what he thought.'

'I think you're mistaken,' said Warrender, still very cool. 'But if you're right and it was indeed intended as a challenge, do you propose to refuse it?'

'No,' said Natalie's father slowly. 'No. I accept—of course.'

CHAPTER SEVEN

NOT until they were in the car on the way home did Natalie venture to mention the *Otello* casting to her father, and then she managed to sound very calm and impersonal.

'I've been thinking of what you said about Laurence Morven wanting to sing Cassio as a sort of challenge to you,' she observed reflectively. 'You know, I don't think anyone in their senses would expect to *challenge* Otello with a rôle like Cassio. It's a relatively small rôle, he's a weak and not very impressive character, and although the music is lovely, of course——'

'One of the real tests of a lyric tenor,' interrupted her father resistlessly. 'Quite important enough for even John McCormack to sing it in his time and make a minor sensation.'

'But do you suppose Laurence Morven is after a *minor* sensation, after what happened in Paris?' she countered, with a touch of nervous impatience.

'He's after a head-on comparison of the two voices, on the same stage and the same night,' replied her father, unmoved, 'otherwise why should he concern himself with what you have yourself just called a relatively small rôle? And don't forget that it's Cassio who is Otello's deadly rival on the stage—at least in Otello's view.'

'Oh, Father, you're carrying things too far!' she protested.

'What things?' he inquired coldly. 'Never underestimate a role like Cassio. I've known tenors build a career on that kind of part. It may not seem outstanding, but *any* part is what you make it. I once played Cassio myself when I was in my twenties, and there are at least three places where you can upstage Otello himself, if you have the right equipment.'

'And what,' asked Natalie, in spite of herself, 'would you call the right equipment?'

'Apart from a lyric tenor voice of genuine beauty? —good looks, real presence, and that certain charisma which makes the audience remember suddenly that Desdemona was once friendly with Cassio. If he can produce all that, then Otello has a real rival on the stage instead of a cardboard figure.'

'And you think that Laurence has all that?' She sounded more eager than she had intended.

'I don't know. But *he* obviously thinks he has,' was the dry reply. And Natalie felt it would be unwise to continue the discussion. Besides, they had now arrived home.

When they entered the house her father went straight through to the studio, late though it was, took out the score of *Otello* and stood by the piano, lightly picking out some chords with one hand. They were familiar enough to Natalie, and she recognised immediately that they were not from Otello's own music. They came from the role of Cassio.

Her father sang a few phrases, half tone but ravishingly and with a subtle suggestion of almost sensuous meaning. Immediately Natalie felt that stirring of her heart-strings which she inevitably experienced whenever he sang any love passage.

'You hear what I mean?' he said, and then he closed the piano again.

And she heard what he meant.

Whether or not Laurence were capable of putting something of that same significance into those phrases she could not tell. But, remembering his Andréa Chénier and his Don José, she had little doubt. And that was the moment when, dismayedly, she accepted the fact that her father could well be right in thinking that the performance of *Otello* was to be a neck-and-neck challenge between the two of them.

She stood there for a moment, not knowing what to say. And then, because she felt she simply *had* to see her way clear, she asked rather stonily, 'Do you expect me to regard him as an enemy from now on?'

'I, my dear?' Her father turned and surveyed her with what appeared to be genuine surprise. 'How you regard anyone is your business, not mine.' But before she could draw a quick breath of relief, he added, 'I merely suppose you would wish to act towards me with some sense of loyalty.'

'Yes, of course,' said Natalie. 'I only ask because, as you know, I'm going to be Wendy Pallerton's bridesmaid, and he's to be best man. It could be awkward if —if we were openly on bad terms.'

'*Bad terms?*' He repeated the phrase distastefully. 'Dear child, you surely have enough social know-how

147

to avoid anything of the sort. Nothing about the situation requires you to be rude or awkward. Quite the contrary. My own invariable rule has always been that the more I dislike a person, the more I exert whatever charm of manner the good God may have bestowed on me.'

Natalie thought of saying that she did not dislike Laurence; she also thought of recalling one or two outstanding instances when her father had departed from his invariable rule. But she realised no useful purpose could be served by mentioning any of this, so she desisted.

It was the next day that she voiced some of what was in her mind and heart. And this time it was to the much more sympathetic ear of Mrs Pallerton.

'Please don't think I'm making any accusations against Laurence myself,' she said earnestly, 'but no amount of argument would make Father budge from his opinion. Naturally he's aware that the position presupposes a certain degree of rivalry, and he has exaggerated this in his own mind.'

'Perhaps he hasn't exaggerated it,' replied Mrs Pallerton unexpectedly.

'Oh——' Natalie looked shocked. 'Do you really think Laurence engineered this situation so that he could—so that he could——'

'Show off his cruelly young voice against the voice of his ageing rival?' finished Mrs Pallerton with frightening candour. 'I don't know, Natalie. Though he's my own nephew. I know him mostly as a person rather than as an artist. He's a good fellow as nephews go,

148

but I'm not quite sure what happens when a very ambitious, single-minded artist has an unusual opportunity offered to him. Laurence *is* ambitious—I do know that. He wouldn't be where he is if he were not.'

'You mean you're on Father's side?' said Natalie curiously, and was surprised to see Mrs Pallerton colour slightly.

'No, I wouldn't say that. It isn't for me to take sides, as you put it. I only say that your father might be right. I earnestly hope he's wrong—but I understand why you feel a little uncomfortable about the situation.'

'You don't understand at all!' thought Natalie. But she managed to say quite naturally, 'So long as there isn't any unpleasantness at the wedding.'

'Why should there be?' inquired Mrs Pallerton, rather as Natalie's father had done. 'People who gather at weddings aren't all necessarily friendly towards each other, but in a civilised community they give the impression of being so.'

'Yes, of course,' agreed Natalie. And she wondered if she were singular in supposing that she and Laurence might find the occasion both difficult and embarrassing.

Everything else concerned with Wendy's wedding seemed to go smoothly. Even Natalie's father appeared to be pleased rather than nonplussed by his own invitation.

'You'll meet Laurence there,' Natalie reminded him quickly.

'Yes, of course. Very kind of Enid to invite me too, but then she is an exceptionally kind and charming woman.'

149

It took Natalie a second to identify 'Enid' as Mrs Pallerton, and then she was surprised, for unlike so many of his younger colleagues, her father was very sparing in his use of Christian names. For some odd reason, she took heart at that. At least her father did not think less of Mrs Pallerton because she was related to Laurence, whatever he might believe of his younger rival's intentions towards himself.

After that, the last week or two before the wedding slipped by very quickly, it seemed to Natalie, and she was curiously unprepared for the slight shock of seeing an excellent newspaper photograph of Laurence arriving at London Airport. The caption underneath stated that he was to act as best man at his cousin's wedding and would also be appearing in the gala performance of *Otello* in which Lindley Harding would be singing the name part.

Somehow, seeing it all in black and white gave it an almost startling sense of significance and reality. But, since no one had at any time appeared to share her anxieties, Natalie kept them to herself.

Then, on the very day before the wedding, Laurence himself telephoned; mercifully, when her father was out. Even so, she was surprised to hear herself say, 'Oh, Laurence, I'm so glad to hear from you!'

'Are you? Then I'm sorry I wasted several days doubting if I should phone,' he replied lightly. 'We're to meet tomorrow, I gather, in specially friendly circumstances, and I was wondering if we were going to let bygones be bygones and forget about our last rather stormy encounter.'

'I was wondering too! And it—it's very generous of you to make the first approach.'

'Well, one of us had to,' he said practically.

'Yes. But it was I who—who——'

'Committed assault and battery?' he suggested.

'Oh, Laurence, I'm ashamed of myself whenever I think of it,' she exclaimed remorsefully.

'Then don't think about it,' he advised her.

'You mean that?'

'I mean it. Where would be the sense of continuing to feel badly about something so silly? We were both under a good deal of strain at the time. And isn't a wedding—even someone's else's wedding—supposed to be an occasion for measureless good feeling?'

'Oh, yes! I'm so glad you feel that way. I was getting ridiculously nervous and self-conscious about it all, and felt quite unhappy.' Thus did she reduce weeks of misery to that harmless phrase. 'Now I can enjoy dear Wendy's wedding as one should.'

'Apart from which, of course, we should have had to come to some sort of truce, shouldn't we?' he went on. 'If I'm going to sing in the same performance as your father I can hardly be quarrelling with his daughter.'

'No—that's true,' she said, but suddenly her lightened spirits dropped. For, incredibly and unforgivably, she had actually forgotten about the *Otello* performance. Now she recalled it with a sense of guilt and unease, for she began to see what might well lie behind this casual peace offer.

'Until tomorrow, then,' he was saying. 'And for my part, Natalie, I'm looking forward to it.'

151

'I, too,' she said, as enthusiastically as she could. Then he rang off, and she was left standing there, the receiver still in her hand, while she tried to decide if her father's loyal daughter should have handled this conversation quite differently.

Not that one could have rejected Laurence's olive branch, of course. Her father himself had expressed himself in favour of pleasant, civilised behaviour. There was hardly anything in what she had said which needed any change, nor was there much in the way she had said it which could be criticised, except perhaps that her tone had been a little over-friendly.

What really pricked her conscience was the way she had *felt*, but no one need ever know about that, of course. She slowly replaced the receiver, as though sealing off the contact with Laurence and everything it implied. But the fact remained that for her the joy of hearing his voice again, uttering words which seemed to put them back on a friendly footing, meant more than anything else which had happened since the quarrel in Paris.

The wedding next day followed the pattern of most weddings. Wendy was perhaps a little less nervous than most brides, her mother less tearful and emotional than many mothers on these occasions, and the bridesmaid found herself wondering how anyone could have preferred the quite pleasant groom to the unfairly attractive best man.

She saw him for the first time as she gravely followed Wendy up the aisle; and it seemed to her that, even in stage costume and at the centre of the scene, he had never appeared handsomer or to more advantage than now, when he was playing second fiddle to the bridegroom.

He flashed her a smile before he turned to carry out his simple duties and, as Natalie stood behind Wendy, listening to the words of the marriage service, she thought a great deal about that smile and rather too little about the bride whose bouquet she was now holding.

What did it feel like to exchange those familiar words with the one person who mattered most in one's life? and how could one assess the importance of any other circumstance—or loyalty—when measured against that thought?

Somehow she had not quite expected to find herself alone in the car with Laurence on the way to the reception, but so it happened, and the sudden intimacy of the situation made her feel shy and as though, after all, she did not know him very well.

He, on the other hand—confident and gay—turned to her and said, 'You're looking gorgeous! Who chose that lovely little Tudor headdress for you?'

'Wendy, I think.' She gave him a quick smile. 'Didn't she look simply beautiful herself?'

'Yes, she did. She's a good-looking girl.' He said that sincerely, but somehow in quite a different tone. 'Do you know the couple who're giving the reception?'

'Only that they're called Colonel and Mrs McEvleigh. They're cousins of some sort on Mrs Pallerton's side, aren't they? Wendy described them as "remote but rich".' Again she gave that slight, tentative smile. 'She said both she and her mother would have preferred something less formal, but the offer was made—kindly but rather firmly—and it would have been difficult to refuse without offence. Besides the fact, of course, that they could give Wendy a much more gorgeous affair than her mother could have done.'

'Well'—he glanced out of the window to see where they were going—'I suppose every girl likes as many frills as possible to her wedding.'

'Do you think so?' Natalie considered that soberly. 'I'm not sure that I agree.'

'How would *you* like it to be, then?' he asked, as though he were really interested to know.

'I—haven't thought about it,' she said, not quite truthfully. 'There are more important things to a wedding than the frills, as you call them. Don't you think so?'

'I? I don't know that I've thought much about it either,' he admitted. But being at a wedding makes one think about weddings in general, I suppose.'

And then the car drew up outside one of the few handsome houses overlooking the Park which are still in private hands.

Their host and hostess, Natalie realised immediately, were much more socially aware—even snobbish—than the Pallertons. Undoubtedly they had organised the wedding reception extremely well, but to Natalie, who had seen a good deal of this sort of thing in her time, it was obvious that Mrs. McEvleigh at any rate was not so much a star-gazer as a star-collector. She immediately swept both Natalie's father and Laurence Morven into her own personal net; and Natalie herself, as a not inconsiderable appendage to her famous father, came in for some gracious attention too.

Presently, on the legitimate plea that the bride might need her, Natalie managed to disentangle herself.

'The place seems full of people I don't know,' she said frankly to Wendy.

'Same with me,' the bride replied cheerfully. 'But then Sarah McEvleigh thinks every social occasion is a chance to gather names and titles under her roof. With Laurence as best man I imagine she's concentrated on stage people, whether or not they're interested in me or Peter. I can tell you, Mother and I didn't send invitations to more than two-thirds of these people. But it doesn't matter,' she added lightheartedly. 'We're the star performers, they're just the supers. Do you, for instance, know any of the people coming in at the moment?'

'No. Do you?'

'Not one.' Wendy shook her head with a laugh, and then added, 'Oh—well—Do you see what I see?'

'Yes,' said Natalie in a small, chilled voice, as into the room came Minna Kolney, superbly dressed, radiantly attractive and apparently very much at home in these surroundings.

Bypassing the bride, she went immediately to speak to her hostess and then she turned to Laurence with a charming little exclamation of what might have been pleased surprise, and kissed him, easily and a trifle possessively, in front of everyone.

'Neither Mother nor I invited *her*,' muttered Wendy before her attention was claimed by other guests. And as she turned away Natalie felt—and indeed looked—strangely isolated and forlorn.

It was her father who came up to her and said conventionally, 'A very charming wedding,' and never before had she been more glad of the security which his slightly overwhelming presence afforded her.

'Yes, wasn't it?' She linked her arm in his, with relief and a sudden rush of affection. And then she repeated once more the phrases about the beauty of the bride, because she could say those without giving her whole attention to the words.

'Very lovely,' agreed her father impersonally, 'but I thought you looked lovelier. You were the real beauty in the church—don't look so startled, even parents pay compliments occasionally. And stop glancing across at Minna Kolney in that surreptitious way. That's what she wants you to do. And he too, I don't doubt. I suppose it was he who engineered her presence here.'

'Who?' asked Natalie faintly.

'Morven, of course. Go on talking to me, it doesn't matter much what you say. Just put a good face on things. One should always look radiant when one has been shocked or rebuffed. Ah, Enid'—he turned as Mrs Pallerton came up—'I was just telling Natalie that I felt quite proud of my daughter, as I'm sure you did of yours. They made a charming picture standing there in the church.'

He seemed to have overlooked the mere bridegroom in the charming picture, but Mrs Pallerton appeared to take Peter's presence as read. She made some graceful reply and then added, with a rueful little laugh, -

'I'm afraid it's all rather more of a social jamboree than Wendy and I intended. I hope you didn't mind being treated as a social capture.'

'My dear, what man ever minded being treated that way?' he replied lightly. 'In any case, it's you I regard as the hostess here, and I'm charmed to be looked on as *your* capture at any time,' he added gallantly.

'I can't bear it!' Natalie was thinking as she stood there smiling suitably and taking what part she could in this light badinage. 'I can't *bear* it. Did he really arrange for her to be here? He looked pleased enough to see her. And she kissed him as though he belonged to her—and he kissed her in return. What else could he do, of course? But he's still talking to her and smiling, and I hate the sight of her—oh, she's coming this way.'

She was, too.

'Why, Natalie, I didn't see you!' She smiled brilliantly, though her tone and glance implied that Natalie was easy to overlook. 'What a pretty little bonnet. So quaint and very much *you*, somehow.' Then she went on with hardly a pause, 'I gather from Laurence—at least I think I do—that you and he have made it up.'

There was not quite a question mark at the end of that sentence, but very nearly so, and she had now cleverly contrived to interpose herself between Natalie and the other two, so that they were more or less on their own. But somewhere in Natalie there was a useful little streak of her father, and suddenly she pulled herself together.

'Made it up?' She gave an amused little frown of puzzlement. 'Had we anything to make up?'

'Well'—immediately there was an edge in Minna's voice—'the last time I saw you two together you'd just landed a hearty slap on his cheek. I had no idea you packed such a punch until I heard the sound.'

'Oh—that?' Natalie laughed. 'It's a long time ago and'—she looked Minna Kolney straight in the eye —'there's been a lot of water under the bridge since then.'

It gave her a fierce sense of satisfaction to see the other girl momentarily taken aback. But Minna recovered herself almost immediately, shrugged and changed the subject to the dangerous one of the coming *Otello* performance.

'So your father and Laurence are to be heard at last in the same performance,' she said musingly. 'It should provide a chance for some interesting comparisons. *Someone* is being over-bold, I would say.'

'Do you think so?' With a thoughtful air, Natalie affected to mistake her meaning. 'I don't think Laurence need be scared. Cassio's part is too small to challenge any comparison with Otello, isn't it?'

'Oh, you're too much for me,' declared Minna, with an unexpectedly good-humoured laugh, which puzzled Natalie until she saw Laurence within a couple of yards of them. 'Come here, Larry, and help me!' Minna still looked charmingly amused. 'I've been trying to defend your decision to sing Cassio in the same performance as Natalie's father, but I only got my fingers rapped for my pains. I don't think Natalie *likes* you and me.'

'That isn't true!' exclaimed Natalie. 'At least——' she stopped abruptly, for she had almost been trapped into saying she couldn't stand Minna.

But Minna caught up the words and laughed afresh. ' "At least——" ' she quoted mockingly. 'You see there are certain qualifications, Larry.'

'I don't know what you two are talking about!' He frowned doubtfully, half amused but not entirely pleased, Natalie saw. And at that moment Wendy came up and said,

'Come with me, Nat, it's time I went up to change. I didn't realise quite how late it was.'

'Just a moment——' Natalie began distractedly.

'Don't worry, I'll explain,' said Minna, with a malicious gleam in her eye. And because there was nothing else she could do, Natalie yielded to Wendy's slight tug on her arm and left the field to her rival. For that was how it seemed to her at that moment.

It was infuriating and frustrating beyond belief. Minna would take every advantage of the situation and undoubtedly remould the conversation nearer to her heart's desire. But this day was Wendy's day, and her one bridesmaid must be at her disposal when needed.

'It doesn't matter,' Natalie told herself fiercely and untruthfully, 'it doesn't really matter. That odious girl was keenly aware of the rivalry there must be in the *Otello* performance—and how can he be less so? They've probably even talked it over, and if that's so, she's welcome to him! I'm on Father's side. I *have* to be on his side! He didn't hesitate to come to my rescue when I needed him just now, and how could I do less than stand by him a hundred per cent when he needs me?'

All the time these confused thoughts were running through her head she was helping Wendy to divest herself of her wedding dress and change into her going-away dress. And then, at the last moment, Wendy reached into a large cardboard box, spilling tissue paper all over the place, and lifted out a superb mink jacket.

'Wendy! How lovely!' Preoccupied though she was with her own thoughts, Natalie could not restrain her admiration.

'Isn't it? I thought perhaps you might have seen it.' Wendy slipped it on and glanced at herself in the mirror. 'Wasn't he an absolute angel to think of it?'

'Peter, you mean?'

'Why, no.' Wendy turned and stared at her friend. 'Didn't you know? Your father had it sent yesterday. Apparently he said something to Mother about my not having a father to do the right thing by me, and could he have the pleasure instead?—You know the lovely period speeches he makes. Mother was almost in tears when she told me. I thought you *knew*.'

Natalie shook her head wordlessly.

'Well, that makes it even nicer. That he didn't tell anyone about it, I mean.' Wendy looked slightly moved herself for a moment. 'He's a darling. They don't come in that pattern any more. Look after him, Nat.'

'I will,' said Natalie slowly. 'Oh, I will.'

And then they both went downstairs. Wendy still carrying her bouquet, to be greeted by the guests surging into the hall, laughing and talking and calling out goodbyes.

There was the usual flurry of kisses and farewells, and then Wendy slipped her arm into her husband's. But she turned once more at the door and tossed her bouquet into the crowd. Unmistakably she threw it in the direction of Natalie, but a hand came up in the crowd, and a moment later Natalie saw Minna Kolney standing there, the flowers clasped to her in both hands, while she laughed up into Laurence Morven's eyes.

CHAPTER EIGHT

NATALIE was not unduly superstitious, but to her there was something disagreeably symbolical in the fact that Minna had reached up and caught the bride's bouquet which had so obviously been intended for *her*. That gay indication that whoever caught the flowers would be the next bride had been Wendy's way of saying, 'Good luck—and may you find someone as nice as my Peter!'

Ordinarily, she would have been no more than amused—or possibly faintly vexed—that she had muffed the catch and lost the bouquet. But that Minna, of all people, should have snatched it away from her and then turned in smiling triumph to Laurence—that was very hard to bear.

Suddenly she felt tired and dispirited, a feeling not unknown to those left behind at a wedding when the central characters have departed. She still contrived to smile and chat and accept gracefully the compliments bestowed upon her, but she was acutely conscious of the fact that Laurence made no further attempt to seek her out.

Quite likely, of course, this had nothing to do with any misstatement Minna might have managed to make. While their duties had kept them together his attitude had been impeccable, but, now that the demands of

162

convention had been satisfied, he might well feel it was no longer incumbent upon him to go out of his way to be specially friendly.

Whatever the explanation, his ignoring her made her feel anxious and unhappy. And she was not sure if she were relieved or sorry when her father suggested they might well make their departure.

'So soon?' she exclaimed instinctively, and then flushed as her father looked surprised.

'At least half the guests have gone by now,' he pointed out, 'and Mrs Pallerton, for one, is looking very tired. I should think she—if not our hostess—will be glad to see the last of us. Weddings can be very exhausting once the principal excitement is over. Did you want to stay for any special reason?'

She could hardly say that indeed she did: That she was disappointed not to have had more conversation with Laurence, and felt that if she lingered there might be a chance to set right whatever Minna might have contrived to put wrong between them.

Instead she said, 'I expect you're right. I'll go and have a word with Mrs Pallerton, and if she doesn't need me for anything I'll'—she swallowed quickly—'just thank Laurence for looking after me and——'

'Did he look after you?' Her father lifted his eyebrows in that way which was so telling on the stage and so disconcerting in real life.

'Well, so far as the best man does look after the bridesmaid,' she explained hastily. 'It's just—a matter of convention.'

'I didn't notice him being particularly attentive,' her

163

father said, and although the statement was made casually she found it extraordinarily wounding. 'But speak to him by all means. There's no need to be unmannerly simply because someone else is.'

Her longing to defend Laurence and his manners was out of all proportion to the occasion, but she somehow controlled herself. To make an issue of such a trifle would only imply excessive concern on his behalf. So she went over to Mrs Pallerton without more ado and found, as her father had predicted, that Wendy's mother had reached the point of just wishing the whole thing were over.

'I'm dead tired,' she confessed, 'and have a horrible feeling that's just how I'm looking too. To be frank, I just want to go home and to bed. I'm sure your father has also had enough of it. He was kind enough to ask if I would join you both for dinner, but even kinder in immediately accepting my excuses. You've been such a support, dear, and he's been wonderful too. Did you ever see anything so lovely as that mink he gave Wendy? I can't get over his generosity.'

'He's very fond of you both, Mrs Pallerton,' Natalie said earnestly. 'I think he's never forgotten how kind you were after that unhappy illness in Paris. You helped to rouse him from quite a prolonged fit of melancholy, you know. One remembers these things very gratefully.'

'I'm happy to hear you say so. And I do hope'—she gave a worried little laugh—'that things don't go badly between him and Laurence. I'm so truly fond of them both——'

'I, too,' interrupted Natalie quickly. 'At least, I mean of course that I'm devoted to Father and—and I like Laurence very much too.'

'Then go and say some nice words to him now,' said Mrs Pallerton. 'Look, he's over there by the window, and unencumbered by Miss Kolney for the moment.'

So Natalie went, and as she came up to him he turned and smiled at her. Not perhaps with the glowing warmth of his usual confident smile, but almost tentatively as though he were a little doubtful as to why she had approached him.

'Laurence, we're going now. I just wanted'—she stopped, because really there was nothing for which to thank him specially, and suddenly she found herself saying instead—'I just wanted to make sure that nothing I said was misrepresented—I mean misunderstood. I had to rush off and help Wendy change from her wedding dress, and I left the conversation rather clumsily unfinished. I wasn't saying *anything* about not liking you. It was just that——'

'Do you like me?' he interrupted flatly, and she caught her breath.

'Yes,' said Natalie, just as simply. And then for good measure she added, 'I just don't like her, that's all.'

'I don't much like her either,' said Laurence. And Natalie thought that was the finest speech she had ever heard from anyone.

'Listen'—he took her lightly by the arm—'can't we go out somewhere together? We've had no time together really, and there's so much——'

'No, I can't. I have to go with Father. He's waiting for me.'

'Oh—Father!' His tone dropped a couple of notes to something like disgust. 'Look, Natalie, you don't really mind that I'm singing with him, do you? It was bound to come to that eventually. And when the performance was first mooted in New York I realised that was the big chance. It suddenly occurred to me that——'

'Don't tell me any more,' she interrupted desperately, 'please don't! I can't bear it—this business of divided loyalties. It makes me feel physically ill.'

'There's no question of divided loyalties,' he told her impatiently. 'The position is a perfectly natural one——'

'I must go, dear—I must go.' She had no idea that she had called him 'dear', even when she saw his expression change.

'All right, my sweet,' he said softly, 'but one of these days we're going to have this out, you and I. Father isn't going to be the big problem in your life for ever.'

She was horrified at what he had said. And even more horrified that she had put herself in a position to hear him say it. Somehow she should have staved off such a speech. Certainly she should never have said anything which gave him the chance to utter such words. For a second she remained there still, poised on the edge of protest and reproach.

Then he said, still speaking softly, 'Your father is coming this way, my dear, and I think you'd better go.'

He relinquished her arm and she went without a word, meeting her father halfway across the room, so that it was not necessary for the two men to exchange more than a distant bow and smile.

'Come,' said her father, putting round her the cape he had just fetched for her, and as she shivered involuntarily he asked, 'Are you cold?'

'I—don't think so.' But she was—both hot and cold, and her father remarked amusedly, 'Well, your cheeks look hot enough, certainly. What brought that flush there? compliments or insults?'

'Neither,' she replied abruptly. 'Let's go, Father.' And, with a curious glance at her, he escorted her from the room and out to the waiting car.

She feared he might ask her more on the way home. But, like Mrs Pallerton, he suddenly looked very tired, so that Natalie remembered with poignant clarity Wendy saying, 'Look after him, Nat. They don't come in that pattern any more.'

And she had said she would look after him. With all that that implied.

The next major event looming up on the horizon was, of course, the *Otello* performance. It was to be a big social occasion, quite apart from its artistic importance, and, inevitably, a certain amount was written about it in the press. With varying degrees of tact or tactlessness, attention was drawn to the fact that two tenors who might be regarded as interesting rivals would be taking part. And one newspaper came out quite frankly with the statement that Lindley Harding would, in a sense, be 'defending his title.'

'What nonsense!' exclaimed Natalie nervously to Charles Drury. '*Otello* is one of the greatest roles in all opera, and Cassio is only a secondary character.'

'Of course,' agreed Charles, rubbing his chin meditatively, 'of course. But you'd do well to keep that particular bit of journalism from your father's notice.' Which she did.

As was usual, she didn't attend the earlier rehearsals; neither her father nor Warrender tolerated outsiders until the performance was more or less in shape. But she did of course ask, as naturally as possible, how things were going.

'Very well, on the whole,' her father replied, just as naturally. 'I'm in good voice, thank heaven, and Anthea of course is beyond praise. The best Desdemona in all my experience.'

'And the Iago?' she inquired, by way of working round to asking about the rest of the cast.

'Excellent. But then he never is anything else. Morven is good too,' he added, without forcing her to inquire about him. 'He plays the part rather as I used to myself, making an alarmingly attractive creature of him.'

'How do you mean—alarmingly attractive?' she asked quickly.

'He doesn't alarm *me*, if that's what you're asking.' Her father smiled slightly. 'But one sees why Otello's jealousy was not difficult to arouse.'

'Then he must be exceptionally good.'

'He is exceptionally good,' her father conceded. 'Are you coming to the dress rehearsal?—you are? Then you'll see for yourself.'

But on the morning of the dress rehearsal he was

moody and difficult, and most unexpectedly said he would rather not have her there. Charles could come with him instead.

'But, Father, why not?' She was terribly taken aback. 'I always come! I was looking forward to it so much.'

'You don't "always come",' retorted her father unreasonably, and not entirely accurately. 'Anyway, you have the performance to look forward to. No, please, Natalie, for heaven's sake'—as she made as though to protest further—'do I have to explain my slightest wish to my own daughter before I can have my own way? I'm nervous and tense enough already. Stop being so selfish, and think for a moment what it means to have to play a part like this.'

She stopped arguing on the instant, of course, but her disappointment was almost unbearable. Not only because she wanted so much to hear him, but because she wanted so much to hear and see Laurence.

Then gradually her disappointment began to give way before a feeling of anxiety. *Why* did he not want her there? Was he afraid that she, who knew his work so well, might detect the fact that he was less than his best? Was that it? Beneath the cool confidence, which had suddenly turned to nervous irritability and unreasonableness, was there a deep, agonising insecurity?

Day after day he had been hearing himself in competition with the fresh young voice of Laurence Morven. What had that done to him? Suddenly a great pity welled up in her, swamping both disappointment and resentment.

'Look after him, Nat. They don't come in that pattern any more.'

If all she could do for him was stay away from that vital dress rehearsal, that was what she was prepared to do. Though she had to wipe away a few very bitter tears at the thought.

Somehow she occupied herself during the long hours of the morning, resisting the almost overwhelming temptation to go to the Opera House and at least walk around outside. In that way she might even have caught a glimpse of Laurence—but that, of course, was not the important thing.

The rehearsal must have gone on until late in the afternoon, for it was five o'clock before her father and Charles returned. Her father went straight to his room without comment, and chilled and fighting something like panic, Natalie followed Charles into the office.

'How was it, Charles?' She was surprised how the words almost stuck in her throat.

'Fine,' said Charles, cheerfully and not very informatively.

'How was Father?'

'Superb. Saving himself a little—as he's entitled to, of course, at a rehearsal. But he got through splendidly. Morven was excellent too. I've never seen or heard such a good Cassio. The whole part came to life in a riveting way. He really is a handsome devil. He makes Iago's task of creating Otello's jealousy almost easy.'

'Charles,' said Natalie slowly, 'why did Father not want me to come?'

'How should I know, my dear?' Charles was glancing through a pile of correspondence as he talked. 'They're

170

all unreasonable on the day of a performance, and some of them are just as bad over a dress rehearsal.'

'He's never been like that before.'

'Perhaps he's never been so afraid before,' replied Charles.

'*Afraid?*' She caught her breath. 'Do you think he was really afraid?'

'Yes.' Charles was no longer fingering the letters in front of him. 'Afraid that you, his own daughter, would find Morven's voice more beautiful than his, and some- how convey that to him between the dress rehearsal and the performance. It would have knocked the bot- tom out of his confidence, you know, and he's going to need every ounce of that confidence to take him through.'

'He couldn't have thought that!' The colour swept into her face and then away again. 'That's something you've thought up on your own, and you're mistaken, Charles.'

'No, I'm not. He told me so.'

'He *told* you so?' There was half a minute of frozen silence. Then Natalie said shakily, 'Father told you that—about me?'

'It wasn't a reproach, Natalie.' Charles spoke rather uneasily. 'It was just the way he thought things might be. And he couldn't risk the nearest person to him showing enthusiasm and preference for the wrong man. This performance is the biggest challenge of his whole career. He's like a man walking on the brink of a precipice—even a small stone in the wrong place could send him over.'

'I wish he'd told me,' Natalie said painfully. 'Oh, I wish he had told me. I could have explained—reassured him.'

'I don't think you could, you know,' replied Charles kindly. 'People with an obsession aren't easily open to argument. And he *has* a sort of obsession about Laurence Morven. He thinks he's set to down him, and he thinks your loyalties and affections are uneasily balanced between them.'

'Do you think that too, Charles?' She looked directly at him.

'My dear, what business is it of mine?' He laughed protestingly. 'I don't know, and perhaps you don't know either,' he added shrewdly.

She did not answer that. But after a moment she said remorsefully, 'And because of what he thought, I wasn't there to comfort and support him.—Oh, I know you were there, Charles, and I'm sure you did everything that a good friend could. But he's the kind of man who needs a woman to make a fuss of him when he's feeling less than confident. Mother used to say that —and she was right.'

'As a matter of fact'—Charles made a note on the side of his blotting pad—'Mrs Pallerton turned up, so the womanly touch wasn't entirely missing.'

'Mrs Pallerton?' A curious little stab of something like jealousy made Natalie wince. But she dismissed the feeling immediately with the self-scorn it deserved. She was glad if such a good friend had been there to make things easier for her father. But if only she could have convinced him of *her* support too. Of course she

172

wanted Laurence to have a big success. But, even more, she wanted her father to be the sensation of the evening.

Even more? Yes, of course! for Laurence had most of his career still in front of him. For her father there could not be an unnumbered procession of triumphs left.

She longed to speak to him about what Charles had told her, longed to assure him of her undivided loyalty. But she realised that any form of discussion on that topic could only upset the fine balance of his security and composure. There was nothing she could do but keep her anxieties and her vague remorse to herself—the hardest thing in the world to do.

On the night of the performance he left for the Opera House an hour or two before her. This was quite usual, particularly when he had an extensive make-up to put on, but she hugged him before he went, with all her heart, and said,

'I want it to be *your* great night, darling. I want that before anything else at all.'

'Sure?' He smiled at her with a good deal of his characteristic humorous charm.

'Absolutely sure,' she asserted earnestly. And he touched her cheek lightly and affectionately, but she heard a breath of a sigh before he turned away and went out to the car.

All the time she was dressing, and on her way down to the Opera House, she thought continuously of him with a sort of tender anxiety. But when she entered Covent Garden—which was decorated for the gala

173

occasion and looked glorious—the indefinable sense of excitement which a gala always engenders began to take hold of her.

Looking round, she saw many people she knew, and she was particularly glad to see that Mrs Pallerton was sitting near her. With a few minutes to spare before the curtain went up, she went over to thank her for having given friendly support to her father at the dress rehearsal.

'I just happened to be there backstage,' Mrs Pallerton assured her. 'Laurence wanted me to bring something for him at the last minute. He was sorry not to see you there, Natalie.'

'I was sorry not to be able to come,' Natalie replied, without offering any explanation of her absence.

Mrs Pallerton glanced at her curiously and then, as though making up her mind about something, said, 'Laurence asked me to give you his love.'

'He did?' Natalie looked startled and her colour rose. 'Just—casually, you mean?'

'No, Natalie. I don't think there was anything casual about it. I think he hoped you would take the message seriously.' Mrs Pallerton smiled, but not as though there were any joke involved.

'O-oh,' said Natalie, and that was all she said, because it was time then to go to her seat. But as she went she thought, 'He sent me his love! But it's a good thing I didn't go to the rehearsal. He might have said something—unwise. And then what might Father not have thought?—But Laurence sent me his love.'

The lights were already going down as she slipped

into her seat, to the sound of the applause which greeted Oscar Warrender's appearance. And then she was, as always, swept away on the waves of storm music, held as it were in the vortex of the tempest, hardly catching her breath until the hurricane had blown itself out and her father made his splendid entrance.

She held her breath once more, but for a different reason this time. She need not have worried, however. As he delivered the tremendous, trumpet-like notes of Otello's first phrases the whole audience seemed to shiver with a sort of ecstatic incredulity. Effortlessly, triumphantly, almost arrogantly he flung those well-nigh unsingable notes into the auditorium, and then strode from the stage as though they had presented no more difficulty than a nursery rhyme.

'The house is his!' Natalie thought, as she sensed the atmosphere around her, and the intensity of her relief and pride brought the tears into her eyes. Indeed, it was minutes before she even realised that Laurence was on the stage.

She saw him first through a mist of unshed tears, so that he seemed to move—lightly, elegantly, romantic-ally—in a kind of golden glow. Even when, yielding to the blandishments of Iago, he became increasingly and dangerously drunk, his attraction was only half ob-scured; and during the ensuing fight he displayed a sort of dashing grace which was breathtaking.

Natalie was not the only one who stiffened with al-most painful anxiety when he stood at last before the angry Otello and was dismissed contemptuously from the scene. It was almost too realistic, she thought—

and then was immediately absorbed in the matchless way Anthea and her father sang the love duet which ended the act.

In the interval she heard someone say, 'This is going to be a night to remember for the rest of our lives!' And then Mrs Pallerton came across to her and Natalie saw she was almost as excited as she was herself.

'He's beyond praise,' Mrs Pallerton said, in a shaken sort of voice.

'They both are,' returned Natalie quickly.

'Yes, yes, of course. But there's no comparison between the two achievements. Laurence is splendid, I grant you; the best Cassio I ever remember. But it's your father who is carrying the full weight of the performance.'

And so it was throughout the evening. Laurence took every opportunity his rôle offered, and sang with a freshness and beauty that was a joy to hear. But hardly ever, in all her experience, had Natalie heard or seen her father rise to such heights. Vocally and dramatically he could not put a foot wrong. Even without the voice he would have dominated the scene by his acting and the sheer nobility and poignancy of his interpretation. But with the voice added—that unique, brilliant, heart-searching tenor sound—he captured and held every person in the audience.

Quite a number of people besides Natalie must have wondered if, at his age, he could still work the magic spell which had put him, and kept him, at the top all these years. That he had done so, and even virtually bettered his own best, constituted the sort of miracle against which no one is proof. It was one of those occasions in which all take part and all feel a sense of personal triumph. Just to have been there seemed an achievement, and the place went wild.

For several curtain calls he refused to come out alone. But in the end Anthea led him on and determinedly left him alone on the stage, to receive the kind of ovation which crowns a whole career. The reward not only of genius—which, after all, is a gift from Heaven—but of a lifetime's work and devotion to one's art.

'He'll never do it like that again; no one could,' Anthea said to Mrs Pallerton, who had joined her now as they stood among the applauding throng. 'It's a once-in-a-lifetime performance.'

'I don't think he ever means to do it again,' replied Mrs Pallerton quietly. 'He told me after the dress rehearsal that if he could score an overwhelming triumph this time, he would probably allow it to be his last Otello.'

'He told you that?' Natalie was astonished that her father should have confided such a thought to anyone but herself. Then she reminded herself that all artists tend to make dramatic prophecies when their nerves are taut. But even so——

'I'm going round backstage now,' she whispered. 'I can see this is likely to last some time yet, and I'd like to be there before the crowd.'

'All right, my dear, you go. I'm staying until the last clap,' replied Mrs Pallerton with a laugh. And Natalie slipped away.

In spite of her good intentions, it took much longer

than she had expected to make her way through the solid crowds who seemed disinclined to move for anyone. And when she reached the pass door she found it barred against her.

'Can't go round yet. No one allowed across the stage,' the unfamiliar man on duty told her.

She thought of asserting her identity and arguing the question, but decided against that. Instead, she made her way out into Floral Street and round to the stage door, where she was greeted more warmly.

'Go on up, Miss Harding. What an evening! What an evening! Your father certainly beat them all tonight. Never heard even him in better shape.'

'Thank you——' she found it unexpectedly difficult to steady her voice. 'I thought he was marvellous too.'

She went along the familiar stone corridor and up the stairs to the dressing-rooms. There was hardly anyone about. But, as she reached the first floor, the door at the end of the corridor leading to the stage burst open, and several of the cast came surging through. They were talking, laughing, singing snatches of the opera— all in a state of high excitement and jubilation.

Her father was not among them, but Laurence was, and she went forward eagerly to greet and congratulate him. He almost held out his arms to receive her, and she would probably have run straight into them. But at that moment her father, almost terrifyingly splendid in his stage costume and with the aura of his success around him, appeared at the end of the corridor alone.

She forgot everything else at the sight of him. She almost thrust Laurence's hand from her, and it was into her father's arms that she ran, clasping him with all the strength of her love and devotion.

'Oh, darling, you were superb!' She hugged him afresh. 'It was the finest thing even you ever did. There's no one like you—no one!'

Her father held her very close for a moment and said nothing. Then she raised her glowing face to him and, as she did so, she saw that he was looking over her head at someone, and on his expressive face was a slight smile of triumph.

CHAPTER NINE

'COME——' Natalie's father said, his arm firmly round her so that she could not turn from him, 'come in while I take off my make-up.'

'Can I just——?' she was pressing against his arm in an instinctive bid for release.

'No,' he told her, and with one of his effective stage gestures, he swept her into his dressing-room and closed the door behind them.

His dresser was already there, making it impossible for Natalie to enter into any passionate argument, even if she had wanted to do so; and certainly it was not for her to spoil the evening's triumph with any paltry dispute.

But *was* it paltry? What had it meant to Laurence that she had brushed him aside, however understandably? And what had he read into the slight smile her father had given him?

'Father, I haven't had a word with anyone yet! May I just go and speak to Anthea and——'

'No, stay where you are, darling.' His tone was affectionately indulgent but quite firm. 'I want you with *me* for a short while. I've seen so little of you in the last few days. It was my own fault, I know—I was jumpy and nervous and no company for my favourite girl.'

Only on very special occasions did he apply that laughing term of endearment to her, but somehow that only stiffened her sudden resolve.

'You thought I might have the bad judgment to find Laurence Morven's voice better than yours, didn't you?' she said, not looking directly at him, but meeting his eyes in the mirror. 'And understandably, you couldn't risk my giving you that impression just before a vital performance. You needn't have worried, Father. Yours will always be the greatest voice in the world for me.'

He smiled at her in the mirror and replied almost negligently, 'But he sang most beautifully tonight.'

'Yes, he did.' She spoke steadily. 'And his idea of the part was splendid. But it was your night in every sense of the term, you must know that. Just as every person in the house knew it too.'

'I don't deny it.' He was still smiling slightly. 'That was how I intended it to be.' With a decisive gesture he peeled off his Otello wig, and ran his hand through his own thick grey hair. 'He hid any chagrin exceedingly well—I'll give him that. But he knows now not to challenge me on my own ground, I think.'

'Father'—she was suddenly overcome by angry indignation, and even the presence of the dresser did not deter her—'you're completely mistaken in what you think. You do Laurence the greatest injustice. If you'd let him speak——'

'I have no wish to hear him speak,' returned her father indifferently.

'Well, I have!' she retorted violently, her mingled

love and anger suddenly sweeping her forward to an iron determination to have the matter out, once and for all. 'I'm going to fetch him—*now!*'

'Natalie——' the authoritative note in his voice was as commanding as at any time during the performance, but for once it failed to have any effect upon her. Avoiding his detaining hand, she made for the door, almost pushing the surprised dresser out of her path. And a second later she was outside in the now crowded corridor.

'No,' she said mechanically to the many inquiries, 'no, he isn't ready yet. And nor is Mr Morven,' she added for good measure, as she beat a peremptory little tattoo on the door of Laurence's dressing-room.

'Yes?' he called out, and then he himself came to the door, and for a brief moment she saw Mrs Pallerton in the background.

'Please come. My father wants you.' She spoke without choosing her words and then saw from his set face that he was on the verge of saying that her father could wait. '*I* want you,' she continued in a low voice. 'It's important—please.' And, looking past him, she said, 'And will you come too, Mrs Pallerton?'

They came then, both of them—puzzled, but sufficiently under the spell of her urgent tone to do just what she commanded. Like her, they put aside all queries and comments from the crowd and accompanied her into the principal dressing-room.

'Please leave us alone for a minute or two.' Natalie was just as commanding to the dresser, who immediately withdrew, leaving Natalie with three puzzled people—two of them rather wary and resentful.

After a moment Laurence, looking across the room with hard eyes at the man sitting by the dressing-table, said coldly but politely, 'What was it you wanted to say to me?'

'I?' Lindley Harding stood up and immediately seemed to dominate the room. 'Nothing, my dear fellow. And I have no more idea what Natalies wants than apparently you have yourself.'

'It's nothing my father needs to say,' Natalie was trembling, but her voice was clear and steady. 'It's something he needs to hear. Laurence, will you please tell him—and me—just why you wanted to sing in this performance tonight?'

'Isn't it obvious?' her father interrupted coldly.

'No, it is not. It's something which needs putting into words for all of us.' That time her voice did tremble slightly. 'Will you please say—*please*, Laurence. Just why did you immediately volunteer to sing Cassio tonight when you heard that my father was to sing Otello?'

'I thought you knew. You wouldn't let me enlarge on the subject at the wedding,' he reminded her a little resentfully. 'You implied——'

'I think,' said Natalie softly, 'that I also had somehow got things wrong.'

'Well——' Laurence hesitated a moment longer, even staring down at the floor in a strangely boyish and awkward manner. Then he cleared his throat and said, 'I guess it sounds naïve and corny, but I thought that if

183

ever one day, I was good enough to sing Otello myself, I'd like to be able to say that I once played Cassio to the greatest Otello of them all.'

He stopped speaking and, except for a sharply indrawn breath from Mrs Pallerton, there was complete and utter silence. Then, as though that silence embarrassed him, Laurence glanced up and met the older man's eyes.

'Didn't you guess that was what it was?'

'No,' said Lindley Harding slowly, 'it never occurred to me. But then I am not, as I now see, such a generous man as you are.'

'Oh——!' breathed Natalie softly. And when her father put out his hand to her, she went to him immediately, and into the circle of his arm.

'I must tell you—Laurence'—he had never addressed Laurence Morven by his first name before—'that my daughter very much wanted to come and tell you how tremendously she—and I—admired your remarkable performance tonight. I rather meanly refused to let her go. I apologise now—and would like her to speak for both of us.'

He released Natalie and gave her a little push towards Laurence. She took a step forward—doubtfully yet hopefully—and then another one. Then he held out his arms to her, and she ran into them and was held and kissed. A long, hard kiss which seemed to dissolve all barriers and misunderstandings.

'I think'—Lindley Harding smiled slightly at Mrs Pallerton, who was standing silently by—'that Natalie has expressed herself very effectively without words.'

184

Then he passed his hands over his face and suddenly looked very tired.

'You'd already cleared the way with any words that were necessary.' Mrs Pallerton touched one of those expressive hands lightly. 'The generosity was not all on Laurence's side.'

He glanced at her and smiled again, a little wryly that time.

'Should I stretch generosity even further, and let *him* take her out tonight?' he said with a slight sigh.

'It would be very kind and thoughtful,' Mrs Pallerton told him. 'Though I must add that the arrangement would leave me without an escort, since I was going to supper with Laurence. But if you liked to take me instead——?'

'My dear, I should be charmed.' He laughed, in a much more relaxed and natural manner. Then he turned to the other two—still in each other's arms and oblivious of anything around them. 'I regret to break up such a romantic scene,' he said, 'but there is an impatient public waiting outside.'

'Oh!' The two started apart and then stood there hand in hand, looking slightly dazed by their own happiness.

'You and I are changing partners for this evening.' Lindley Harding put a hand on Laurence's shoulder. 'Enid is kindly accompanying me to supper, and I think you and Natalie have a good deal to say to each other, so take her along with you.'

'Oh, thank you!' Still dazed, Laurence put up his hand over the one that rested on his shoulder. Then he looked down at Natalie and said, 'Come, darling.'

She was so unutterably bemused and happy that she actually turned and went a few steps with him before she remembered. Then she left him and rushed back to her father.

'Thank you, darling, darling Father!' She reached up and kissed him once or twice in a quick, breathless way.

'For what?' He looked down at her with half amused tenderness. 'For nearly losing you your Laurence?'

'No. For—for giving me to him without rancour.'

They looked at each other fully for a moment—she pleading for the completeness of the surrender, he characteristically holding for a moment longer to his supremacy over her.

Then he took her face between his hands and kissed her.

'*Senza rancor,*' he said, and smiled, before he once more gently pushed her towards Laurence.

She went with Laurence after that. Through the impatient crowd once more, to wait only a very few minutes outside his dressing-room before he re-emerged to receive congratulations and good wishes and dispense some graceful, pleasant acknowledgements. Then, hand in hand once more, they went down the stairs and finally out at the stage door.

Here there was an enormous crowd, who greeted Laurence with enthusiasm, while one or two people, recognising Natalie, asked 'Is Mr Harding going to be long?'

'I don't think so.' She smiled, because she felt she

loved everyone and could smile at everyone that evening.

'We hope not, anyway, because we ourselves are waiting to cheer him,' asserted Laurence.

'*Are* we?' Natalie turned to him in laughing surprise.

'But of course.' Laurence stood there, smiling and handsome and gloriously sure of himself. 'He's earned everyone's cheers tonight.'

'Oh, darling Larry, thank you,' she whispered, as they moved to one side and stood, like any two gallery fans, waiting for the great man to appear.

It was another ten minutes before he came, but she was not cold because Laurence's arm was round her. And when she heard the excited murmur round the doorway, and saw the ripple of expectation moving through the crowd, she too pressed forward, for the first time in her life outside, and not inside, the magic circle which surrounded the extraordinary being who was her father.

'He'll be alone!' was her immediate thought, and it brought an uncontrollable ache to her throat.

But he was not alone. Enid Pallerton was with him, standing a little behind him, and smiling as though she found the position of companion both moving and exciting.

There was a great cheer—led, Natalie realised suddenly, by Laurence. And then her father stood there, as so often before, signing programmes and autograph books and exchanging a few gracious words with his devoted public. It had always been one of his best rôles, she recalled with loving amusement.

187

'When is your next *Otello* performance?' someone asked boldly.

'I couldn't say.' Smilingly he drew a firm line under his signature. 'Perhaps this was the last one.'

'Oh, *no*!' There was a concerted shout of protest from the crowd.

'Well, take heart.' He looked amused. 'Most of us have more than one farewell, remember. But'—suddenly he looked across to where his daughter stood with Laurence Morven, and Natalie realised that his quick glance had taken them in from the beginning—'there'—he indicated Laurence with one of his most eloquent gestures—'is your future Otello.'

There was laughter and some clapping for Laurence at that.

'And when you stand round this stage-door to cheer him,' Lindley Harding went on, 'some of you will remember and say, "We heard him sing Cassio once. And the Otello wasn't bad that night either!"'

And, taking Enid Pallerton by the arm, he went out to his waiting car.

Did you miss any of these exciting Harlequin Omnibus 3-in-1 volumes?

Each volume contains 3 great novels by one author for only $1.95.
See order coupon.

Violet Winspear

Violet Winspear #3
The Cazalet Bride (#1434)
Beloved Castaway (#1472)
The Castle of the Seven Lilacs (#1514)

Anne Mather

Anne Mather
Charlotte's Hurricane (#1487)
Lord of Zaracus (#1574)
The Reluctant Governess (#1600)

Anne Hampson

Anne Hampson #1
Unwary Heart (#1388)
Precious Waif (#1420)
The Autocrat of Melhurst (#1442)

Betty Neels

Betty Neels
Tempestuous April (#1441)
Damsel in Green (#1465)
Tulips for Augusta (#1529)

Essie Summers

Essie Summers #3
Summer in December (#1416)
The Bay of the Nightingales (#1445)
Return to Dragonshill (#1502)

Margaret Way

Margaret Way
King Country (#1470)
Blaze of Silk (#1500)
The Man from Bahl Bahla (#1530)

Available only by mail!

40 magnificent Omnibus volumes to choose from:

Great value in Reading!
Use the handy order form

Elizabeth Hoy

Snare the Wild Heart
(#992)

The Faithless One
(#1104)

Be More than Dreams
(#1286)

Roumelia Lane

House of the Winds
(#1262)

A Summer to Love
(#1280)

Sea of Zanj (#1338)

Margaret Malcolm

The Master of
Normanhurst (#1028)

The Man in Homespun
(#1140)

Meadowsweet (#1164)

Joyce Dingwell #2

The Timber Man (#917)

Project Sweetheart
(#964)

Greenfingers Farm
(#999)

Marjorie Norell

Nurse Madeline of Eden
Grove (#962)

Thank You, Nurse
Conway (#1097)

The Marriage of Doctor
Royle (#1177)

Anne Durham

New Doctor at
Northmoor (#1242)

Nurse Sally's Last
Chance (#1281)

Mann of the Medical
Wing (#1313)

Henrietta Reid

Reluctant Masquerad
(#1380)

Hunter's Moon (#1430)

The Black Delaney
(#1460)

Lucy Gillen

The Silver Fishes
(#1408)

Heir to Glen Ghyll
(#1450)

The Girl at Smuggler's
Rest (#1533)

Anne Hampson #2

When the Bough Breaks
(#1491)

Love Hath an Island
(#1522)

Stars of Spring (#1551)

Essie Summers #4

No Legacy for Lindsay
(#957)

No Orchids by Request
(#982)

Sweet Are the Ways
(#1015)

Mary Burchell #3

The Other Linding Girl
(#1431)

Girl with a Challenge
(#1455)

My Sister Celia (#1474)

Susan Barrie #2

Return to Tremarth
(#1359)

Night of the Singing
Birds (#1428)

Bride in Waiting
(#1526)

Violet Winspear #4

Desert Doctor (#921)

The Viking Stranger
(#1080)

The Tower of the Captive
(#1111)

Essie Summers #5

Heir to Windrush Hill
(#1055)

Rosalind Comes Home
(#1283)

Revolt — and Virginia
(#1348)

Doris E. Smith

To Sing Me Home
(#1427)

Seven of Magpies
(#1454)

Dear Deceiver (#1599)

Katrina Britt

Healer of Hearts
(#1393)

The Fabulous Island
(#1490)

A Spray of Edelweiss
(#1626)

Betty Neels #2

Sister Peters in
Amsterdam (#1361)

Nurse in Holland
(#1385)

Blow Hot — Blow Cold
(#1409)

Amanda Doyle #2

The Girl for Gillgong
(#1351)

The Year at Yattabilla
(#1448)

Kookaburra Dawn
(#1562)

Complete and mail this coupon today!